"What do you want?" Chrissy asked

"I wondered when we'd get around to that." Rodrigo paused, giving her the once-over. "What do you think I want?"

She flushed at the suggestiveness in his tone. "I'm sure I don't know."

"No, I'm sure you don't. I certainly don't want what you seem to imagine I want." His blue eyes moved lazily over her.

"You flatter yourself if you think you can read my mind," she retorted.

"It might not be so interesting, even if I could," he replied dismissively. "It's no doubt full of the usual fantasies held by females such as yourself."

"What would you know about *my* fantasies?" she flashed back, her lip curling.

He gave a gleam of a smile. "It doesn't take a genius to guess your game."

SALLY HEYWOOD is a British author, born in Yorkshire. After leaving university, she had several jobs, including running an art gallery, a guest house and a boutique. She has written several plays for theater and television, in addition to her romance novels for Harlequin. Her special interests are sailing, reading, fashion, interior decorating and helping in a children's nursery.

Books by Sally Heywood

Harlequin Presents first edition March 1992
ISBN 0-373-11441-9

Original hardcover edition published in 1990
by Mills & Boon Limited

JUNGLE LOVER

SALLY HEYWOOD

jungle lover

Harlequin Books

TORONTO • NEW YORK • LONDON
AMSTERDAM • PARIS • SYDNEY • HAMBURG
STOCKHOLM • ATHENS • TOKYO • MILAN

CHAPTER ONE

THEY seemed to have been tramping through the rain forest forever, thought Chrissy, as she stumbled along the narrow path behind the porters. The atmosphere was like a steam bath, making her long blonde hair stick in damp tendrils around her heart-shaped face. On all sides the endlessly tall trees blocked out any hint of sky, drowning them in a sepulchral gloom that hour by hour began to arouse all kinds of primitive fears in her.

Stop it! she scolded herself as a liana coiled snake-like over her shoulders, making her jump. It's your own fault you're here, she admonished. There's no one to blame but yourself! But the relentless, echoing shrieks of parrots and monkeys and the multitude of un-nameable and possibly dangerous creatures fifty metres above their heads in the canopy played on her nerves. It wasn't only the liana hanging from the branches of the giant evergreens, long and sinuous in browns and acidic greens, and threatening in its similarity to the cobras and pythons of her imagination. It was the sheer vastness of the place, its ominous, watchful presence that seemed to set the little group of travellers at nought.

When her guide, Pedro, announced a stop not more than five minutes further on, she couldn't help quick-ening her pace. He turned with a smile as they came suddenly into a grove of sunlit grass. Chrissy blinked green eyes in the strong light and shook out the damp blonde hair, running sticky fingers up through the roots and longing for a long, cool shower.

Pedro got the men to spread out a tarpaulin for her. 'We siesta here for one hour, then it is but one hour more to the river-bank.'

'The last leg! Thank heavens for that! So we should definitely be there by nightfall!'

The guide came to stand beside her. He only came up to her shoulder, but what he lacked in height he made up for in bulk. 'Beautiful, isn't it?' he observed, following her glance around the grove.

Chrissy nodded. Despite her fears of imaginary pythons and the more real dangers from insects, spiders, bats and the species of poisonous plant that Gavin had warned her about, she couldn't help agreeing that there was a savage grandeur about the place. It was still wild and untamed—and threatening for that very reason. She gave a tremulous smile. 'To tell you the truth I feel a little bit dazed. Gavin briefed me very thoroughly before I came out, but it hasn't prepared me for the real thing!'

'Maybe you should have stayed in the city longer to get used to the climate,' he sympathised.

Chrissy thought longingly of the café-lined streets and squares she had left the previous day.

'You're probably jet-lagged as well,' Pedro went on, regarding her tired face. 'It is a long flight from London, no?'

She nodded, then lay down on the tarpaulin, too exhausted to talk. She would try to snatch a nap as best she could in the sticky heat, as Pedro advised.

She tossed and turned uncomfortably. Her cotton shirt was clinging to her skin and she loosened the top three buttons when she realised Pedro and the three porters had already closed their eyes. It allowed a brief cooling draught of air to finger inside before quickly turning to sticky heat again. It was the air itself that pressed its clammy hands over her, and even when she wafted her soft-brimmed bush hat over her heated skin it made little difference to the way she felt. Even wearing the absolute minimum, no bra, just a shirt and cotton trousers over the briefest of cotton panties, she felt as if she were melting in the heat.

If only I could get rid of these trousers, she thought. They were long, heavy-duty cotton, and seemed to cling to every curve of her thighs, but a glance at Pedro and the three bronzed young men carrying all the equipment showed her the folly of that idea. It would look provocative to say the least! She shuddered. Despite Pedro's protection she didn't feel safe at all.

At least she could loosen the laces on her jungle boots and wriggle her toes. She didn't dare take them off in case something attacked her while she slept. If she slept.

Defiantly shutting her mind to the dangers all around, she forced her eyes closed. But her mind was buzzing with the newness of everything. She was lucky to have got this assignment. The man she was taking over from, Gavin, had warned her it would be tough. But she had wanted the challenge. She had wanted to show them that even if she had accidentally won that ridiculous beauty contest she was a career girl first and foremost, a serious person, not just an empty-headed doll. She was somebody who was going to make her mark.

Even so she couldn't help opening her eyes now and then to give a quick, frightened glance around the grove. The porters seemed to be asleep, sprawled like three puppies under a tree. Pedro lay beside her, eyes shut, breath verging on a gentle snore.

To think I was in rainy old England three days ago, she thought. It was overwhelming. It was as if she'd landed in paradise. Ever since they had left the city, scene after scene of astonishing beauty had unfolded before her and now they were in a setting fit for the first day of creation.

Through half-closed lids she watched the sunlight shaft through the velvety shadows beneath the noisy green canopy overhead. Despite her fears and a mind filled with new sights and sounds she must at last have dozed off, for eventually she felt herself struggling from out of a deep slumber broken only by random dreams.

The air was still steaming, heavy with the pungent odour of tropical blooms, and as her eyelids flickered she saw Pedro, still sleeping on the tarpaulin beside her. But the second thing she saw was a pair of unfamiliar jungle boots on the other side of him.

Her green eyes narrowed sleepily, trying to make sense of what they saw, for attached to the boots was an endless pair of khaki-clad trousers.

As her sleep-bleared eyes shifted upwards they alighted next on a thick leather belt. It was buckled over unfamiliar slouching hips. Moving up inch by slow inch, her now startled glance encountered a khaki army shirt, straining to sheath the muscles of a broad, masculine chest. The shirt gaped at the neck, revealing a deeply tanned throat. Then her head tilted as she emerged from sleep, befuddled senses registering a strong jaw, jutting cheekbones, a smudge of shadow beneath two piercing eyes. They were now smiling sardonically down into her own.

She gave an exclamation of mingled surprise and fear. The muscles in her stomach clenched and she managed to raise herself on to one elbow.

But for the eyes, she would have guessed she was looking into the face of a South American, but they were a pair of eyes of the coolest, iciest shade of cobalt she had ever seen.

A violent fear invaded her. She became shudderingly aware of the fact that she was virtually alone, lying unprotected on the tarpaulin in a remote part of the rain forest—at the mercy of a complete stranger.

Just looking at him reawakened all the fears she had been trying to repress. He towered over her, giving an exaggerated sense of height and authority. She could see he was taller than average and formidable in a very physical way that sent shivers of warning up and down her spine. The moment in which he went on gazing down at her seemed endless . . . and, now the initial shock had worn off, all she could do was stare dumbly up at him like a cornered animal.

In that moment she felt she learned every last thing about him.

She raised herself again, resting on one hand. The way his blue-eyed glance lasered over her defenceless body, coming back again and again to her face, told her he felt the same thing—he had stripped her. She lay naked before him. She saw him give a predatory half-smile. There was no humour in it. Only triumph. Arrogance. Certainty. But certainty of what?

She shook her head to clear it. It must be the heat pounding her with such wild fantasies!

But the man standing over her was no fantasy—he was all flesh and blood and naked aggression.

She brushed a hand over her face in confusion, then sat up properly, wishing Pedro would wake up and save her—but even as the thought flew into her mind she knew a man like this could annihilate the little man with the flick of a wrist if he felt like it!

Her glance dropped to the stranger's wrists. Strong, tanned, sprinkled with black hair, they rested casually on his leather belt, fingers looped in the top of it. He was a man very much at ease with himself, though something about the angle of his head told her he was always on the alert. He must be a warden of some sort, she hazarded, taking in the tough, no-nonsense jungle boots, the rifle slung over one shoulder, the air of being in the place where he belonged.

But his silent and entirely insulting regard had gone on long enough. 'Who are you?' she croaked, unsurprised to find her voice out of control. She sat up, drawing in her legs. 'What are you doing here?' she asked more strongly, failing to disguise a note of accusation. Her glance automatically skidded to the scientific equipment the bearers had been portering—supplies for the research post. He didn't look like a thief, but what did she know? He could be one of the cut-throat bandits that were said to roam the area. In fact, it was more than likely!

He must have read her thoughts. In return he gave a humourless chuckle. 'So, angel, how long are you going to last out?'

His voice was a rough drawl that made Chrissy's toes curl. Resenting the ease with which he seemed to be asserting his dominance over the situation, she scrambled on to her knees, but the temperature defeated her and she faltered for a moment, swaying in the oppressive heat.

Now she was kneeling at his feet—it seemed to emphasise her subjugation, but, fight it as she would, the humidity was lapping round her, making her limbs tremble and the stranger's shape swim before her eyes. For a helpless moment all she could do was crouch at his feet, looking up at him, unable to gather the strength to bring herself to stand face to face with him. The heat was simply overwhelming, like being trapped in a steam bath.

When he saw her momentarily beaten he made a gesture with one hand as if to assist her to her feet, but as she automatically raised her hand in response he abruptly withdrew his own and stepped back, narrowing his eyes. 'What's the matter?'

'It's so hot,' she muttered, longing for a cool shower and a drink of something chiming with ice cubes.

'You shouldn't be out here if you can't take it,' he retorted roughly. 'It's no place for tourists. This isn't a pleasure ground.'

'I can take it.' She wanted to deny that she was a tourist—how dared he?—but the effort was too much and all she could manage was to draw herself up as best she could while crouching there at his feet. She dared not risk making a fool of herself any more by trying to get up but she could show by her expression that she wasn't beaten yet.

'Get everybody on the move,' he ordered, ignoring her efforts. 'It's time you left. It'll be nightfall before you know what's hit you.'

With that he began to make his way across the clearing. She saw him heft the rifle more comfortably over his shoulder. His broad back clearly told her he expected to be obeyed on the instant. It whipped up her antagonism as much as the curt order that had issued from his lips. He reached the edge of the clearing. Multi-coloured parrots flew shrieking from the undergrowth at his approach.

She made a final effort and got to her feet, then drew in a breath. 'What the hell's it got to do with you when we move off?' she shouted across the grove after his retreating back.

She hadn't expected much reaction, but her words acted as if he'd been roped. He stopped dead then turned slowly to face her. His expression plainly said he wasn't used to having his orders questioned.

He gave her a slow, insolent scrutiny, cold blue eyes tearing her fragile confidence to shreds. She felt the hairs on the back of her neck prickle alarmingly but she braced herself for a whiplash reiteration of what he'd just said. Instead, he merely raised two sharply drawn brows in an expression of mock amusement. It plainly showed he regarded her comment as beneath contempt.

His lips, she noticed hazily in the second in which they outfaced each other, were full and sensual, but now, together with the raised eyebrows, they expressed nothing so much as the surprised contempt he obviously felt— as if amazed she could actually speak, let alone contradict him.

She felt herself bristle but controlled any outward signs of anger. She wasn't going to let him know he was getting under her skin. She knew the type. It would only make him worse! 'Well?' she demanded, raising her own arched blonde brows in a mirroring of his own response. Her chin rose too and her cupid's bow lips visibly tightened.

'It's cause and effect, my sweet angel.' His drawl was scathing. 'You won't reach the river until nightfall if you lounge around here all day. I don't know who's supposed to be in charge——' he glanced at the still recumbent Pedro, and then across at the sleeping porters before peering towards the forest as if genuinely expecting someone else to appear—Chrissy knew it was a pantomime designed to put her in her place, '—but,' he went on after he'd drawn out the pause as long as possible, 'they sure as hell like waiting for trouble.'

Despite his manner, his words gave her a jolt and she realised that she was supposed to be in charge of the group—at least, it was up to her to tell Pedro when and where she wanted to go. Maybe this annoying stranger was right to offer advice. Even so his manner irked her. He had no right to saunter around reprimanding complete strangers without even bothering to find out who they were!

'Do you always barge in handing out advice right, left and centre?' she demanded with a lift of her chin. Before he could answer she went on, 'It so happens I was about to get everyone on the move again when you came up.'

His amused smile told her he didn't believe a word of it. 'Just do it, then. You've been well out of things for the last ninety minutes, catching up on your beauty sleep no doubt. One of you at least should have stayed awake. I take it,' he went on smoothly, 'you've had this jaunt of yours cleared by the appropriate authorities?'

'What?'

'Well?' He knew she'd heard him and his reply showed he thought himself above having to repeat anything.

Chrissy bit her lip. Nobody had mentioned any clearing authorities to her. It was obvious he must be a ranger. One of that officious breed of people who liked everything docketed before they allowed anybody to make a move.

She curled her lip. 'I'm sure you're only doing your job. Congratulations. If I ever bump into your boss I'll let him know how efficient you are.' She half turned with the intention of nudging the still sleeping Pedro awake with the toe of her boot, but the ranger was coming back.

'I don't like gawping tourists,' he told her. 'Where are you supposed to be heading?'

Chrissy drew back. Although a good two yards separated them his nearness was like a physical assault. 'I don't know why you should imagine I'm a tourist,' she clipped. 'I'm here on important scientific work, actually.'

He gave a deep-throated chuckle. 'Really?' Plainly he didn't believe her.

'I'm a botanist,' she said, 'though why I should have to explain anything to you——' She broke off.

His eyes were lasering over her face with a hardness that his apparent amusement did nothing to hide. It made the words freeze in her throat. He broke the silence when

he rasped, 'If I want explanations, honey, I'll get them.'
There was a pause. 'You understand me?'

Hackles up, she tried to match his glance but faltered
at the last minute. 'Mind your own business,' she muttered, clenching and unclenching her fists.

'But it is my business.' Unconsciously he shifted the
rifle resting on his shoulder. Chrissy didn't know whether
it was meant to be a subtle warning. Suddenly she was
trembling again. He moved closer. 'Now I'll ask you
again. What the hell are you doing here?' His voice was
so low she had to strain to catch his words, but there
was no mistaking the hint of menace in his tone.

It forced a reluctant answer from between her lips.
'I've told you,' she croaked, 'I'm a botanist. I have a
perfect right to be here. If there's some bureaucratic
arrangement whereby you're supposed to be informed
about the movements of people through the forest——' that's reasonable, she registered '—then it looks
as if there's been a cock-up. It's not my fault. The foundation is supposed to see to all the details.'

She risked a glance into his eyes and was astonished
at their sudden concentrated glare. 'You mean you're
supposed to be taking over from the chap who went
sick?'

She nodded. At least he seemed to know something.

'You?' he asked again, not trying to disguise the note
of incredulity in his voice.

'Why not me?' she flared quickly. He had unwittingly
touched a raw nerve and she knew exactly what was going
through his mind. It was the old story. 'I suppose you
imagine only men can be botanists? Just because I'm a
girl you think I'm too stupid or something——'

'Not at all,' he came back. 'It's just that——' he
paused, sifting his words carefully '—I'd unconsciously
built up a different picture in my head... You look
nothing like the sort of bearded scientist I was expecting!'

He gave a small smile, tightening the skin over his cheekbones in a way that was suddenly breath-stoppingly attractive. Chrissy's lips opened. 'I must say,' he went on before she could speak, 'it makes a vast improvement to the landscape.' He gave a smile obviously meant to charm.

It roused her hackles again. 'You're all the same,' she clipped back. 'You never get beyond the surface. I'm here to do some serious work. My job means more to me than anything.' Even here, she was thinking furiously, even though this man didn't know she'd won that infernal contest, even here they assumed because she was a reasonably attractive blonde she was some sort of dumbo.

'Keep your hair on,' he remarked casually. The remark only added to her fury, but she gave a shrug as if she couldn't care less what he thought.

'I can assure you,' she said coolly, 'I always do keep my hair on.' Good job he couldn't tell how frightened she'd been coming through that jungle of swinging creepers and howling animals! It would be different when they reached the research station, set as it was in primary forest.

'Been out here before?' he asked abruptly.

She shook her head.

'Don't push yourself too much at first. You'll only exhaust yourself.'

'Will I?' She heard the sarcastic edge in her voice but couldn't change it, it was already out.

She saw his lips tighten.

It was his own fault if he made her sound ungrateful for his advice. He seemed to think she was a complete dimwit—at least, he had such an air of confidence, of authority, it stood to reason he must think that.

But her glance was pinned to his lips again. There was something about them, their soft mobility, their sheen, their promise, she realised with a gulp, that was making her pulses race. She steadied herself. The last thing she wanted was any distraction from work—and certainly not in the shape of a man like this who—— She bit her lip, cutting off the sudden teeming and unbidden images of what a man like this could do if...

He seemed to loom closer. 'What's wrong?' he asked bluntly.

She put up a hand as if to ward him off. 'N-nothing,' she managed to whisper. 'It's just so hot here and...' She glanced down at the sleeping form of the guide. 'I suppose I'd better wake him.'

'Do that.' The ranger was curt again. 'You've lost precious time arguing with me.' With that he slid into the thick wall of vegetation on the rim of the clearing and vanished from sight.

Of all the cheek! thought Chrissy when he'd gone. The very air seemed charged with the man's magnetism. He certainly had presence, she would give him that— but it was wasted out here, she told herself crossly. He should be in films, or running some political party or other. Something that demanded charisma. She could just see him riding at the head of an armed band, astride a white horse... Stop it! she warned herself. The reality was he was a nasty customer—bossy, interfering, very possibly dangerous—and so arrogant he didn't even try to hide his arrogance!

She bent down and shook Pedro by the shoulder. When he woke up she didn't mention the stranger, but instead suggested they get a move on. He rose dazedly to his feet, and within a few minutes the group was back on the track.

The sun was already slanting towards evening when they eventually came out on to the river-bank. They had followed the single-line track for the last hour, the one the stranger had taken, and when they didn't catch up with him on the way—unlikely, thought Chrissy, as he was the type to push himself to the limit whatever the physical discomforts of the climate—she fully expected to see him waiting for a craft to take him up-river. But she was relieved to see no sign of him.

The paddle-steamers came several hundred miles inland from the sea-port but they didn't come as far up as this. She knew they would have to travel the last part of their journey by canoe.

Gavin had described the journey in detail. 'A dug-out,' he had told her, 'can take up to a dozen people, plus baggage. Forget the little canoes you see in the Wild West Park! These are the real thing.'

Now Chrissy saw what he meant. But it only made her even more puzzled as to why the stranger had already left.

The canoes were like water buses. Already there were several people waiting beside an assortment of goods. A couple of hens in bamboo cages pecked at the specks of grain a group of dark-haired children were pushing through the bars for them. She wondered if they were travelling in the same dug-out. They were. She watched in trepidation as the porters loaded the provisions for the research unit, wondering if the narrow craft could really bear such a load. Pedro beckoned. 'Time to embark!'

Shadows were purpling ever thicker beneath the branches of the trees by the time they came in sight of a wooden landing platform jutting out into the water. Suddenly all was movement and noise as one of the men threw a length of twine up to a boy leaning over the edge and everybody prepared to disembark.

When Pedro tapped her on the shoulder she was already stretching her cramped limbs. There were plenty

of willing helpers to hand up their equipment, and as
soon as everything had been stacked on the landing-stage
she climbed up after them.

Unable to help herself, she cast an anxious glance over
the faces in the crowd as if expecting that unforgettable
one to be among them, glowering down at her as she
climbed up. Thankfully her attention was diverted when
she noticed a couple of Europeans in the throng. One
of them came towards her.

'Welcome, Christine!' He raised a hand in greeting.
'Good journey I hope?' It was a sandy-haired man of
around thirty-five.

'You must be Hans Bergdorf!' exclaimed Chrissy,
recognising him as the supervisor Gavin had described
to her.

'Indeed. And this is my colleague Pierre Martin,' he
gestured to the small, dark-haired man standing beside
him. 'The others are preparing a sundowner at the main
house. We've been awaiting your arrival with interest.
And now I can say we greet you with delight.' He took
both her hands and bowed over them. Gavin had warned
her that Hans pretended to be something of a womaniser,
but nothing she couldn't handle. He was a gentleman
first, he had added with a twinkle. A fine scientist, who
would be her number one friend.

Chrissy now turned to greet Pierre. 'Another good
guy,' Gavin had reported. 'His wife is attached to the
unit too. She's a professional photographer. You'll like
them both.'

Not used to having her mind made up for her, she
couldn't help feeling that, on first sight at least, the two
men were just as Gavin had described. A few minutes
later she met Eloise, Pierre's wife, and Lars, the final
member of the small group, as they stood on the steps
of the veranda that ran round the side of a large wooden
house in the clearing.

'You won't get two words out of Lars,' Gavin had warned. 'He's a zoologist and frankly I think he prefers feathered birds to the human kind.' Gavin had concluded by telling her she would have to be prepared to work alone much of the time as everyone else was busy with their own research. 'Social life is a bit monotonous, but you'll get used to it soon enough.'

'I'm not going for the social life,' Chrissy had told him primly. 'I'm going in order to further my career.' She had ignored the gleam of disbelief in Gavin's eye. It was a reaction she had become used to ever since she'd won that infernal contest!

Now she gazed round with a contented smile. A welcome aperitif had been pushed into her hand at once, and she leaned on the balustrade with it clutched in her hand, almost too weary to take a sip. The nice thing was they all seemed to know how she was feeling. 'It's quite an introduction, isn't it?' observed Hans. 'We've all done the same journey ourselves.'

'Probably dinner then bed would be your favourite plan tonight?' suggested Eloise. 'Not that other nights are so very different!' She was a tall, attractive red-head, and when Chrissy had first caught sight of her she'd wondered how she managed to cope with the climate with such sensitive colouring. That had been one of her own major worries. With her own pale blonde hair and delicate skin she couldn't have chosen a worse place to spend the next six weeks from a beauty point of view. She shook herself. It simply added to the challenge. It made her even more determined to win through.

She allowed Hans to usher her into a long low room in the middle of the wooden house. Rattan blinds hung over two windows at the back, clacking slightly in the evening breeze as the earth cooled after the sun had released its hold. Already the sky had darkened in the short time it had taken to walk from the landing-stage to the house, and several oil lamps shed a soft glow over the simple décor. A scattering of bamboo armchairs and loungers and a good-sized dining table were all the room contained.

'I'll show you where to wash,' murmured Eloise, prising her away from Hans. 'These men! I'm sure you'd like to freshen up. Run a comb rather than the mere fingers of one hand through your hair!'

She took Chrissy by the arm and led her down a short corridor. Its floor of polished wood creaked as they stepped along it. The air was rich with the scent of night blossoms, their perfume released now the heat of day was over.

'This is paradise on earth,' murmured Chrissy sleepily, trying in vain to stifle a yawn. 'How are you ever going to tear yourself away?'

Eloise gave a soft smile. 'I doubt whether we'll come back after we leave at the end of the year,' she admitted. She gave a glance down at her tummy. 'I wanted to have the baby out here, but Pierre has become suddenly cautious at the thought of fatherhood. Who knows?' She smiled gaily. 'It is ages yet. He may become devil-may-care all over again when the novelty has worn off!'

Chrissy chatted interestedly to Eloise about the baby and about what it was like to live so far from all the facilities of a city which she had so far taken for granted. Then they returned to the others.

Pedro was to stay for a day or two until the water bus returned from further up-stream and Chrissy was just in time to hear Hans ask him if he'd met García Montada down-river.

She saw Pedro shake his head. There was a small silence and she was about to mention the man they had met down-river when dinner was brought in and conversation turned to other topics. The others wanted to know how Gavin was progressing in hospital and all about her job at the medical research lab back home.

'What brought you out here, Chrissy? You know it's tough,' probed Hans.

Chrissy nodded. 'I know. That's why,' she replied succinctly. Then, seeing from his expression he wanted more, she felt compelled to tell him all about the beauty contest that she had been dared to enter one mad day after finals when a group of them had buzzed off in somebody's ramshackle old car to the nearest seaside resort.

'We wanted to let our hair down, but,' she grinned, 'I'd no idea I'd get roped into something like that!' She flicked a strand of hair back from her face. 'I couldn't believe my ears when they said I'd won! It meant television appearances, photo-calls, champagne parties— that summer before my exam results came out was one long party. I went along with it because I hadn't got a job—my interview with Cavendish at the lab had gone off well but I knew he wouldn't take me on if my results were poor. In a way the contest took my mind off the grim weeks of waiting.'

'Weren't you tempted to continue in the beauty business?' asked Eloise.

'Heavens no! After all those years of studying? I couldn't just throw it away like that!' She didn't elaborate on the background to it all—the childhood when her mother, left in the lurch by an irresponsible husband, had had the struggle of bringing up two children alone. Chrissy remembered those years clearly, how her mother had resumed the studies that marriage had interrupted and, by juggling two part-time jobs with her classes, had eventually managed to qualify as a doctor. Chrissy had made her mind up at the age of ten that she would never land herself in a situation like that—she would make sure she always had the possibility of earning her own living at her fingertips should the necessity arise.

But she was sleepy now and, recognising this, Hans and the others let her go. Soon she was sliding down under the mosquito netting that hung over her sleeping platform. Too tired to take in her surroundings, she plunged at once into the total black-out of sleep.

CHAPTER TWO

NEXT morning Chrissy couldn't remember getting into bed. The last hour or so before turning in was just a haze. Someone—Eloise, she supposed—must have helped her. Certainly when she awoke her clothes were folded neatly and she could see her travel bag safely stored on one of the shelves across the room. There were no cupboards, she noticed, looking round. A row of hooks on a rafter supported half a dozen empty metal coat-hangers. There was a small mirror on the wall, a spindly bamboo table and straight-backed chair and that was it. Spartan lodgings, she thought. But the food had been good last night, though she had been too befuddled with exhaustion to notice what it was.

She lay in the half-light beneath the misty fall of the mosquito netting with the unfamiliar sounds of the rain forest drifting around her. The day was still cool and she decided to start work as soon as possible.

Just for a moment, though, she wanted to relish this, her first morning in the forest. She listened to the raw sounds of wild animals beyond the perimeter of the compound and tried to identify them without success, then she lay there letting her thoughts drift, reluctant to let the moment go... Unfortunately the more awake she became the more her thoughts kept slipping back to that brief encounter the day before.

She could hear his voice, with its seductive accent and the deep bass of his laughter. If only he hadn't been laughing at her! A picture of his lips swam before her

23

eyes, taunting and enticing. She flung the light cotton sheet back with a gesture of annoyance.

It was no good lying here dreaming of a man she wouldn't want even if he came to her on bended knee! For all his sexy charm he just wasn't her type, and if he knew she was daydreaming about him it would merely add to his arrogance. His manner showed her he was entirely used to getting his own way in everything. His facile compliments showed which way *his* mind worked!

She padded across the room to get her bathrobe and sponge-bag.

Gavin had instructed her in what he called the mopping-up operation here, and she would make the lab her first port of call this morning, sort out the unfinished work on his bench, then hopefully be in a position to plan her schedule for the following weeks. Later, if there was time, she would explore the forest—or at least she would try to follow the plan marking out Gavin's finds. Then there were drawings to be done, photographs to be taken. She was going to have her work cut out in the short period available. Certainly there would be no time for daydreaming!

She was looking forward to getting on with it, she realised as she showered in the cubicle down the corridor and slipped into a clean shirt and pants. Everything seemed to have gone without a hitch so far and the people she would be living with were a good bunch. She brushed out her long pale hair and began to coil it up in a way that would feel cool during the heat of the day.

When she was ready she went out into the corridor and made her way towards the welcome smell of coffee. There were far more important things to think about than jungle predators—especially if they came in the shape of a handsome khaki-clad ranger with a gun! Ahead lay a wonderful six weeks.

The housekeeper, Senhora Suarez, turned with an ample smile as Chrissy came into the kitchen. It was a large, airy adjunct to the house, the whole of one wall opening on to a balcony where, Chrissy saw, breakfast was to be taken. As she practised her few words of Portuguese she glanced across at the wooden refectory table and saw that someone had already had a cup of coffee. Senhora Suarez came on to the balcony and removed the cup without explanation before setting down a fresh one for Chrissy.

'No one else is up yet,' she told her surprisingly. 'Senhor Bergdorf is usually the first. You are taking Mr Bartlet's place?' When Chrissy nodded, the woman went on, 'A very nice man. He would try to be out before Hans—friendly competition. You have won this morning!'

Chrissy smiled. 'And I didn't even know I was competing!' She tried to explain that it was excitement at being somewhere new that had dragged her so precipitately from her bed. She hoped she wouldn't disgrace Gavin when the novelty wore off! Quickly dealing with breakfast, she went down the steps towards the long wooden building that had been pointed out to her from the veranda the previous evening. It was kept locked and Senhora Suarez gave her a key of her own when she told her what she wanted to do.

She peered into the bright, orderly room. Benches on both sides with additional islands for special tasks made it look adequate for the work she had on hand. She walked between the counters and the shelves, past Hans's collection of beetles, the specimens, drawings and photographs and the graphs and wall-charts, looking for Gavin's space. Then, undisturbed by anyone, she settled down to sort things out.

She had been working steadily for about half an hour when the door opened, making her turn with a smile of welcome on her lips. A screen in front obscured the entrance and she laid bets with herself on whether it was Hans or Lars who had come in.

Then she gasped. A rapid beating of her heart took her by surprise, but some atavistic fear had already grabbed hold of her. It wasn't the friendly German, nor the silent Norwegian—it was someone quite different . . . She half rose and groped for the back of her chair.

'Please . . .' The newcomer spread his hands with a harsh growl and gestured for her to remain seated—as if she'd been getting to her feet as a sign of respect for him! Already he had covered the intervening distance and seemed to tower over her. 'I don't wish to drag you away from your work . . .' he began, and although the words were innocuous enough his tone seemed to convey the exact opposite to what he said, reducing her research to the level of a mere hobby.

This annoyed her. 'You?' she squeaked, still stunned, and before he could continue she demanded, 'What are you doing here?' Then she bit her lip, annoyed at betraying the same antagonism that his presence had aroused yesterday when they had clashed for the first time.

He frowned, the blue eyes narrowing. 'You seem to imagine I owe you some sort of explanation for every move I make,' he murmured in a throaty drawl. She could detect some slight accent but couldn't place it. His English was good. He must be English, she told herself. But what was he doing here? Gavin hadn't mentioned anyone else with the right to walk about the lab as if they owned it!

'I have a right to know who you are,' she told him as coolly as her bumping heart would allow. 'This property belongs to the foundation. As far as I'm aware there are only five people with the right to come in here—apart from a cleaner or two——' She broke off as he gave a harsh laugh.

'I can assure you, Miss Baker, I am no cleaner——'

'In that case,' she cut in, ignoring the fact that he somehow knew her name, 'perhaps you would account for yourself?'

'*Deos!* We have struck lucky this time! A proper little commandant!' He looked meaningfully down at her feet in their small jungle boots. 'Complete with regulation footwear too, designed to tramp over anybody who gets in the way...' He laughed again, huskily self-confident, but despite the show of humour his eyes were cold with contempt.

Chrissy wanted to hit him. How dared he laugh at her? 'You still haven't explained your presence,' she remarked, sharpening her tone.

He stepped back. 'And do you seriously imagine I'm going to...? To *you*?'

She briefly dropped her glance. Was there nothing she could threaten him with? She lifted her head at once. 'Does Mr Bergdorf know you're roaming around the lab like this?'

The stranger shook his head, still chuckling. 'You're suggesting I go and find him just to let him know?'

For a moment Chrissy wasn't sure how to proceed. 'Well,' she floundered, 'I'm sure it's not usual to have unofficial personnel wandering about in here!' She sounded pompous even to herself, but he brought it out in her and she couldn't help it. She added, 'There are all kinds of things that could go wrong if the whole world could just barge in whenever they felt like it.'

'The whole world?' he intoned poetically. 'Imagine the whole world coming to us!' Then he raised his black eyebrows with a mocking expression which made her feel stupider than ever.

'You know what I mean!' she exclaimed, flushing. 'That door is supposed to be kept locked when no one's in here, for very good reasons——'

'But it wasn't locked, because someone was here, namely you, so what's all the fuss about?'

Briefly she wondered if locked doors would keep a man like this from going anywhere he wanted. But she lifted her chin and said, 'You're just beating about the bush. What do you want?'

'I wondered when we'd get around to that.' He paused and gave her an up-and-down look. 'What do you *think* I want?'

She flushed at the suggestiveness in his tone. 'I'm sure I don't know,' she replied, sounding as flustered as she looked.

'No,' he said shortly, 'I'm sure you don't. I certainly don't want what you seem to *imagine* I want.' His blue eyes lazed without expression over her flushed skin until she felt thoroughly assessed.

'You flatter yourself if you think you can read my mind,' she retorted. With an effort she had managed to stem the flood of heat that betrayed her embarrassment at the images he was summoning up, and forced herself to look collected even though her hands were gripping the back of the bench behind her where his glance couldn't probe.

'It might not be so interesting even if I could,' he replied dismissively. 'It's no doubt full of the usual hackneyed fantasies of a female such as yourself.'

'What would you know about my fantasies?' she riposted with a curl of her lip.

He gave a gleam of a smile, a flash of cynical blue, but didn't rise to the challenge. 'It doesn't take a genius to guess your game,' he rejoined offhandedly.

She gave a theatrical sigh. 'I have work to do. When you leave would you make sure the door is properly closed?' She turned back to the work-bench where Gavin's notes were stacked, waiting to be deciphered, and was about to slide into her seat when a brown hand came firmly down and slammed the file shut.

'You have appalling manners,' he rasped.

She gazed down at the back of the hand on the bench in front of her. The nails were short, well cared for, and on one finger, the wedding finger, was a broad gold band with a small crest on it.

'Well, aren't you going to argue about that as well?' His voice sounded just above her right ear. She dared not turn to face him because it would have brought their faces within touching distance. She could already feel his hot breath on the back of her neck. And she was wrapped in the heady scent of something like vanilla. She still did not turn, so he was forced to look at the back of her head. Eventually he would tire of this baiting and go back to the jungle where he'd come from. She waited. His hand still lay firmly on top of her notes.

After a pause she saw it lift and she half turned, sure he was getting the hint at last, but as she swivelled she found her breasts skimming the wide bulk of his chest just below the fourth button of his khaki shirt, and as her head came up in surprise she swayed, caught off balance. Their bodies matched length for length, his muscled thighs pressing her slim ones, her hips, his pelvis, his chest, her breasts, skimming and parting and, as if accidentally, skimming again, fitting together like the two parts of one whole. Then he very pointedly stepped back. For a moment neither of them spoke. His eyes had iced over once more.

In a daze she saw the sensual lips hovering on a level with her forehead. 'You lose no time at all, do you?' he murmured, scarcely moving them. 'First Pedro. God knows who last night. Now me. Where do you notch them up, on your bedpost or on a scalp-belt?'

'What? I...' She gazed at him, unable to frame a suitable sentence.

'If I catch you behaving like that with the staff again you'll be off this compound quicker than greased lightning, get it?' His lips scarcely moved, the threat like a wisp of smoke, scarcely there.

She must have misheard, she told herself. 'I can't imagine what you're implying,' she managed to stutter. '*Pedro?* What on earth can you mean?'

'Don't play dumb.' His eyes swept over her face, freezing the denial that sprang to her lips. 'You must know I saw you lying blatantly together in the grove yesterday—and you can't tell me the buttons of your blouse came undone accidentally!' His lip curled.

'I beg your pardon!' At last Chrissy managed to rouse herself. 'Are you suggesting I had designs on Pedro?'

'On any man by the way you flaunt your wares. Heaven knows, *I* haven't given you any encouragement.'

'You're the most arrogant, deluded man I've ever had the misfortune to meet——' she began, drawing herself up. She could feel the blood pounding at her temples. '—*if* I was interested in anyone it certainly wouldn't be a—a——' She struggled to find a word both wounding and accurate.

'Yes?' he breathed, leaning dangerously close. 'A what?' His lips hovered near as if actually willing her to resist him!

She felt herself sway as if compelled by an inner force to reach out for him, but she resisted the impulse, her upper lip curling as she strained away from him. Green eyes opened defiantly, outfacing him—it was a deliberate, provoking challenge, screaming the message that what her blood was commanding her to do was nothing but a lie.

He couldn't know that his presence was making her knees as weak as cotton wool. She gave him the benefit of one long, unblinking, emerald glance. 'A louse,' she said through frozen lips. 'And definitely not one of my favourite insects!'

He seemed to lean even closer, taunting her self-control and in an almost-whisper quizzed incredulously, 'You're trying to say you prefer overweight men of five feet two, to someone——'

'Someone like you?' she arched her back, trying to draw herself up and widen the distance between them at the same time.

But her scorn made no impression, his response only to let the chipped ice of his glance dagger slowly over her heated skin in a deliberate provocation. Like knife-points it touched her face, her chin, her neck, then sank down over the collar-bone and inside... How could a glance penetrate inside her clothes? she asked herself in a fever of confusion, as the pinpricks teased her in ever-increasing intimacy, seeking every secret hollow till she wanted to scream for him to stop.

At last, when the tension was almost unendurable, he lifted his head with its mane of thick black hair reaching to his collar, and for a split second she imagined he felt as mystified by what was happening as she was. Then a lazy smile broke over his features. 'No,' he breathed, 'my first guess wasn't off the mark. Given the choice it's obvious where your preference lies...and it's not with our worthy friend Pedro—even though you obviously don't mind if he samples the goods from time to time.'

Without thinking, Chrissy did something she had never done before. She slapped a man across the face.

As the crack of her palm against his aristocratic cheekbone rapped out she was already bringing one hand up to her mouth in dismay. Words of apology sprang at once to her lips but she choked them back. They would be lies. She was *glad* she had slapped his arrogant face after what he had just said! But even so... If she could have retreated she would have. Unluckily there was nowhere to go.

She pressed back further against the work-bench, her whole body trembling with trepidation at the thought of what he might do next.

His face, registering first shock, adopted an expression as blank as a wooden mask. It was worse than if it had twisted in anger. Cold fury was unpredictable where good honest rage was not. But his self-control was formidable.

He didn't even sound angry when he eventually spoke. It was as if her action was beneath his notice—he belittled her by ignoring it. He said in matter-of-fact tones, as if unaware of the livid colour over-printing the deep tan of one cheek, 'Come over to the house at eleven. Hans has gone up-river. You need some information if you're going out into the forest.'

'From *you*? Information from *you*?' she managed to croak. 'You're the *last* person I want information from, thank you very much.' Nothing would entice her to the house without the presence of the others.

But as she glanced wildly round the lab she realised it was as isolated here as it would be on the other side of the compound. When he had gone she would lock the door. He was looking at her with open dislike by now. It made him even more like the predatory jungle animal he had seemed yesterday—with that close, watchful, narrow-eyed glance, judging her motives— wrong though his conclusions turned out to be!

'I can only assume,' he said teasingly as he gazed down at her, 'that you imagine your book-learning somehow makes you immune to the dangers of the forest.' His lips narrowed. 'Your self-confidence verges on the ridiculous.'

She flinched. How dared he call her ridiculous just because she wasn't kowtowing to him? Who did he think he was? He was nothing but a jumped-up forest ranger. She longed to let him really have it, but knew she would be laying herself open to immediate retaliation. She guessed she'd already got away with more than anybody ever had done before!

Forcing a more humble note into her voice, she said, 'I expect I've got a lot to learn, but I'm quite capable of doing the job I've been sent to do without special help. And as for Pedro, you must see what a ridiculous idea it is to think I'd be interested in him. I mean...' She began to flounder under the coldness of his raking glance and, instead of accepting what she said, he gave a hard laugh.

'Not good enough for you now you realise there are richer pickings to be had?' He swivelled, face tight with contempt. 'Suit yourself whether you come across. I'm sure any one of the men will be delighted to fill you in on all you need to know.'

He left, silently, swiftly, like an animal leaving the scene of its latest kill. Chrissy slumped against her work-bench. Why did she feel she had been mauled by a lethal predator? Despite his insults she had won that round, hadn't she?

As she bent over Gavin's notes once more she knew in her heart of hearts that neither of them had won any-thing. They had both lost. But what it was they'd lost she didn't know.

Eleven o'clock came and went. She was dying for a drink as the humidity intensified, but she made do with water from one of the taps, praying that it was safe, and utterly determined that nothing would induce her to face that man again. She didn't even know his name. And still he hadn't told her by what right he could order everyone around!

By midday, though, even she had to give up. It was like working in a steam bath, the end of any real work

for a few hours until the sun started its daily slide to the
west—as the air cooled she would be able to snatch a
few more hours in the lab. Gavin's notes were difficult
to read. His handwriting was so small. She moved slowly
back across the compound with the beginnings of a
headache.

Senhora Suarez was in the kitchen. 'Goodness me, my
child, you missed your break this morning, and now you
are looking so pale!' She bustled forward as Chrissy
entered. 'The men are already in the dining-room. Go
quickly and join them. It is quite informal.'

Chrissy dragged herself through into the next room.
Hans and Lars but, she was relieved to note, no dark-
haired cynic, were seated at the dining-table. They greeted
her jovially and she was soon absorbed by their discussion of the morning's activities. Pedro had accom-
panied Hans up-river and came in a few minutes later.
He gave Chrissy an odd look when she accidentally
caught his eye and she wondered if the stranger had
expressed his suspicions about their activities to him as
well. She could imagine Pedro's reaction! He would be
as astonished as she was!

Waiting for a lull in the conversation so that she could
mention that morning's unpleasant encounter, she had
to hold her tongue until Hans had finished ribbing Lars
about something that had gone wrong the previous week.
When there was a pause she asked, 'A man came into
the lab this morning——'

'I know. That was García Montada.' Hans was shov-
elling food into his mouth. 'I intended to introduce you
before I left, but he tells me he passed you and Pedro
on the track down-river yesterday?'

Chrissy opened her mouth to reply but Pedro cut in,
'Too true. He told me in no uncertain terms this morning
I was a no good sonofabitch for not keeping a proper
watch over Miss Baker.'

It had been Chrissy—or Missy—yesterday. Chrissy scowled and was about to remind him of that fact when he went on, 'I gather he introduced himself to you while I was asleep?' He gave her a reproachful glance and she realised he was put out that she had apparently withheld this piece of information.

The molehill seemed to be turning into a mountain. Chrissy said, 'He didn't exactly introduce himself. He simply strode up. Ordered me to get everyone on their feet, then strode off again. Talk about high-handed! And I'm sorry I didn't mention it, Pedro. It hardly seemed worth it.' She paused. 'I mean,' she went on, 'one minute he was there, the next he wasn't. I didn't realise you knew him.'

'"Know him" is perhaps an exaggeration,' muttered Pedro. He appeared to be mollified by her explanation, however. 'You had complaints about the trip?'

'Of course not!' Before she could quiz him as to whether this was the impression García Montada had tried to create, Lars got up.

'Ah, yes,' smiled Pedro. 'Siesta time.' He and Lars went over to a table on the veranda and she saw Lars bring out a pack of cards.

'García Montada came over to the lab to put you in the picture, did he?' questioned Hans.

'He certainly did!' she exclaimed with feeling.

Hans laughed. 'What's the matter? Surely you're not going to tell me you're immune to *El Senhor*?'

'You must be joking!' Chrissy came back. 'That macho type has no appeal for *me*.'

'You must be the only woman on earth to hold that view! It must be quite a shock for him.' He chuckled with rather malicious amusement. 'He was certainly intrigued to hear we'd got a beauty queen among us!'

'You never told him? Oh, Hans, how *could* you?' She looked at him aghast. 'Now he'll never take me seriously.' She paused. 'Not that it matters one jot, of course. It's just that I hate being patronised by these macho-men who think they can pigeon-hole me.'

'I'm sure he'll soon realise his mistake,' he said affably. He got up. 'Must take my siesta now. I suggest you do the same. You mustn't try to work through the afternoon. This heat's a killer. Ignore those two over there,' he pointed to the card-players. 'They'll play for a while then turn in like everybody else.'

'It seems strange to be sleeping during the day,' she remarked as she followed his example.

'You'll get used to it.' Hans gave her a friendly smile then disappeared towards his quarters.

Chrissy made off in the opposite direction, where her own room was situated. It would have been nice if Eloise had been around instead of out with Pierre somewhere. The two of them shared one of the palm-roofed huts in the compound but they were obviously not 'at home'. She needed to have a good heart-to-heart with someone. That man—that García Montada—made her feel like spitting flame!

So that was his name, she told herself when, after sponging her heated body with cold water, she lay naked underneath the mosquito netting. He must be Spanish or Portuguese, she thought, with a nickname like 'El Senhor', but she couldn't tell which from the pronunciation. Trust Hans to cut him down to size! But if he was Portuguese, she mused, why did he have such incredible blue eyes? She frowned. And *why*, she asked herself, am I wasting so much time thinking about him?

She turned over on to one side. It was impossible to feel comfortable in this heat. It was like a Turkish bath with the heat full on and no way out. Would she be able to last the course? She *had* to. If she didn't succeed she would let down not only herself but all the people who had helped her over the years. And her mother, although she wouldn't say anything, would inevitably feel regret that all her sacrifices had been in vain.

She wriggled about on the bed, her body feeling as if it were turning into a pool of ghee like the tiger in the children's story, except that instead of soft gold her skin was pearly, still winter-coloured.

Wondering how she could get a tan and at the same time find a breath of air, she got up, dragging on a voile shift in misty blues and pinks. It was refreshingly cool against her over-heated body, and she left it unbelted so it floated behind her as she went on to the veranda outside her room. There she found a rocking-chair. Dragging it into a slant of sun on the corner, she looked round for something to use as a fan. Spying a low bush of coconut-palm, she decided one of its thick fronds would be ideal, but she would need a knife to cut it.

Silence lay over the whole house as she made her way to the kitchen. The two card-players had long since gone to their quarters and even the kitchen itself was deserted. She went in and looked around for something she could use. There was a rack of knives on the far wall. Barefoot, she padded over the polished plank floor, and was just reaching up for one when there was a hiss of sound behind her. She swung, the knife firmly in her grasp, then froze.

CHAPTER THREE

CHRISSY'S senses seemed to have sharpened and she was strongly aware of the pungent aroma of unfamiliar spices from somewhere behind her. Outside from within the jungle canopy a bell-bird made a regular sound like the smash of a hammer against a broken anvil. It was piercing and insistent, full of the sense of time ticking by. But the sound that was loudest was the motor-kick of her own heartbeats. She lifted a hand to her throat and, as if recognising that she was cornered, she pressed back until the kitchen work-bench dug into her thighs.

García Montada strode into the room like a conquering war-lord.

At once Chrissy felt a primitive fear, the fine hairs at the nape of her neck rising helplessly as her eyes darted from side to side searching in vain for a way of escape. His electrifying power seemed to reach out, paralysing her will.

'I'm not doing anything wrong!' she blurted. His blue eyes raked her pale form.

Aware that beneath the voile shift she was completely naked, she crossed her arms in front of her, unwittingly pulling the diaphanous material more tightly across her breasts. Her nipples seemed to harden at the contact. She let her hands slide to her sides. García Montada observed these small actions with the piercing blue of a compassionless glance.

None of her movements seemed to escape him, not even the sharp rise and fall of her breath as she lifted her face to him.

38

He gazed down with his head on one side as if weighing the prudence of several courses open to him. Then before she could flee he reached out to grasp the wrist holding the knife. Without removing it from her grip, he forced her hand behind her back and, as her body arched, pulled her slowly and deliberately into his hard, hot body.

Chrissy had no time to do more than open her lips in the beginnings of a protest when his mouth ravaged down over her own. Her breath was stopped, her senses beginning to dizzy.

Despite her initial aversion at being taken so decidedly into the arms of a man who was still almost a stranger, she felt the betrayal of limbs turning to silk beneath his touch. Her mouth moistened instinctively as his tongue began its exploration, at first with a kind of savage hunger then with a slower, deeper, more sensual touch, a more and more pronounced pleasure communicating itself to her so that she could feel her own breathing deepen and become as ragged as his own. The air all around was hot and moist and filled with the thunder of their pulsing blood. Her hand, still holding the knife, came up languidly of its own accord, with his fingers still braceleted around her wrist, then somehow her own fingers were running helplessly through the deep gloss of his hair and the knife clattered on to the floorboards somewhere between their feet.

His embrace became savage. It was like a contest, a battle, desire sweeping them both in a suddenly released torrent towards the precipice of lost control...

It was Chrissy who struggled to her senses first. The sound of the knife falling, the pirating of her mouth by his, the greed of his touch over her moist nakedness, bit by bit jerked her back to reality, sending her hands sliding down his chest to push feebly at first then with greater force against the immovable wedge pinning her against the wall.

His voice was a soft snarl when he saw what she was trying to do. 'Not entirely unexpected——'

'What?' she managed to croak.

'Entice and repulse... you like the teasing game? You like to spice up your inevitable surrender with a little charade of hard-to-get?' He laughed huskily against the side of her blonde head. 'All I have to do is lay bets with myself on how soon you'll say yes...' He lifted his head and looked down at her through narrowed eyes. 'Very soon, I should say... very soon indeed.'

He was still breathing raggedly, his lips hovering just above her own, and he made a feinting movement as if about to possess hers again, but then drew back just as she herself moved away. He brought his lips close to hers again just as she relaxed and then they both withdrew at the same moment. Cat and mouse. Tiring of the game, he brought one hand up to grip the back of her head and, cupping it in a firm grasp, pulled her, resisting, tight-lipped, towards him, until only a few centimetres separated them. 'Soon... yes?' he breathed. 'Siesta with me... in your room? Now? Why not now? Say yes!'

She lowered her lids. She could feel his hard maleness, unashamed token of arousal, burning against her abdomen. When he ran his hands down her spine he massaged as if applying warm oils to it. The scent of him seemed to carry his essence deep into her soul. To herself she groaned with astonishment, I desire this man, this man of all men. But why, why?

To him, too astonished by her own reaction to be angry, she said, 'Don't. I'm not that sort of girl. Let me go.'

His face registered no expression. 'Of course you're not. You're a nice girl. A respectable girl. You don't like to make love.'

Chrissy wasn't breathing any more. 'Let me go,' she said tonelessly, ignoring the irony in his voice. Her breasts were taunted by the muscular movements of his broad chest and she longed to feel his touch on them, to suffer the release he could bring from the wild pain of longing, so shocking in the swiftness of its arousal. But she held herself still in order not to betray the unreason of her desire. 'Let me go,' she repeated like an automaton.

'Of course...' But he didn't move.

'Let me go, please,' she said again in the same flat tone.

'All in good time.'

'Please...'

'We can go to your room.'

'No!'

Still he held her. She could feel his manhood straining to subsume her. If she struggled, she thought, it would push him over the edge of control—sending herself, too, over the edge... It would take the smallest movement. The tiniest, single, most innocent tremor would send them over on to some other, wilder shore where restraint meant nothing.

'I want you to let me go. I'm asking you please to release me,' she repeated, her voice blank with the effort to control the tone of yearning struggling to be expressed.

She could scarcely say more. Her throat felt blocked with desire, the inner voice screaming, Take me, I want you. But it was a voice of impersonal lust. She knew that. It was knowledge she could hang on to, something that would get her safely through the next few months if she could only hold it like a talisman before her. No man had ever made her feel like this. She was bewildered by it.

He was staring into her eyes and something seemed to be exchanged as if they were passing each other on a journey down the corridors of each other's souls. In another moment she would be drawn beyond the point of turning back. She closed her eyes. She tried to set herself against him. He saw the change, knew he had lost her for the moment. Shutters came down over his own eyes. His lips tightened.

She felt his touch withdraw. His body drew away, the heat subsided, her breath came back. She had to clutch the edge of the table for support.

He would have been white-faced but for his deep tan. From across the kitchen he looked at her long and hard without speaking. She still felt enwrapped in his embrace. Still the imprint of his hand marked her flesh. It was against all reason. They didn't even *like* each other. Something seemed to have caught them in its spell. With a shuddering breath she pressed the back of one hand to her forehead and closed her eyes again.

'Are you all right?' He didn't move towards her, but his eyes didn't leave her face.

She lifted her glance and felt the power of those cobalt eyes on hers. She turned, abruptly bending to retrieve the knife. Not looking at him, she said, 'It's so hot. I'm not used to such heat.'

'It's the humidity. You should rest as much as possible to begin with.'

'I haven't time to rest——' she broke in nervily. 'Gavin left so much work to be concluded.'

She stole a glance at him.

'Drink plenty of water,' he told her, his eyes never leaving her face. 'Haven't they told you that? You'll feel better.'

He sounded as if—no, she brushed her hand across her face, again feeling it come away damp. He didn't care. It was just the husky seductiveness of his voice that gave the illusion of concern...

'I was going to make a palm fan,' she told him.

'That's what the knife was for? I thought it was meant for me.'

She gave a shaky laugh.

'I'll get us both water.' He reached to a shelf, took down two pint glasses and filled them at the water-cooler in the corner, approaching just near enough to hand one of them to her, then moving back again to the opposite side of the kitchen.

She sipped at it, feeling trapped, like an animal being scrutinised beneath glass. They were talking to each other, using words of the most ordinary kind, as if nothing had happened. What did he expect her to do next? Carry on like this as if her nerves weren't screaming for some sort of catharsis?

He was observing her as if he felt he was in for a surprise. She was weak with the tide of desire as it ebbed, taking with it all her reason. She could sink to her knees on the wooden floor. She could fall at his feet.

Unable to bear the tension any longer, she measured the distance between herself and the door. It meant she would have to pass close to him in order to escape. 'Thank you for the water,' she said and, clutching the glass between two clammy hands, made a dash for it. He let her go. She hurried along the corridor with her breath held until she reached her own room and closed the door with a sharp snap. Gone was any idea of going out on to the veranda.

She went over to the double doors that gave on to it and closed them, adjusted the shutters in the bottom panels until they allowed in air but no light, and, draining her glass, she slid under the mosquito netting on to the bed. The memory of his kiss seared through her mind. The whole incident had taken maybe no more than five minutes. But it burned in her like everlasting hell-fire. She couldn't forget the way his mouth had felt, ravaging her own, or the way his body had seemed to call to hers, and the look in his eyes, and the way he had slowly released her and then tried to talk to her as if nothing had happened when all the time they both knew as if it had

been shouted aloud that something terrible had taken
hold of them both.

And surely, surely, she thought, there could be no
going back? There could be no backward trail from this
point?

Only when she heard movement from the other side of
the house did she dare rise, dress, and emerge, with
caution, like someone peering out from a shelter after
the passing of a hurricane. Knowing there was no
avoiding what lay ahead, she forced herself to walk down
the corridor towards the sitting-room. The aroma of
coffee already filled the air. When she went in Lars and
Hans were sitting outside in the shade of the veranda
and Senhora Suarez was pouring coffee. She poured a
third cup when she saw Chrissy.

'Did you manage to get forty winks?' asked Hans.

Chrissy shook her head and tried to look nonchalant.
'It was too hot.'

'You'll be used to it by the time you have to leave,'
he joked.

'I thought I'd try to fix up a fan of some sort,' she
said. All the time she spoke she was wondering if García
Montada was going to saunter on to the veranda. If he
did, what would she do then?

But Hans was answering her. 'There's an electric fan
somewhere around.'

'I thought we tried to conserve electricity as much as
possible?' There was only a small generator for
refrigeration.

'Can't have you suffering!'

'I saw a fan in a film once,' she admitted, trying to
shut thoughts of Montada from her mind. 'It was a
simple palm-leaf affair, tied to a string which was in turn
attached to the foot of a rocking-chair. Whenever

anybody sat in the chair the slightest rocking motion moved the fan.'

Hans laughed. 'Sounds a good idea.'

Chrissy gave a shaky smile. 'As soon as I've had a session with Gavin's notebooks I'm going to make one.'

Soon she was back in the lab. It looked as if she would have the place to herself most of the time. Eloise and Pierre had still not returned, and she had forgotten to ask where they were. It seemed almost too hot to make conversation. Maybe tonight after dinner it would be different. Last night she had been simply too tired to stay up. García Montada seemed to have vanished from the face of the earth.

The pattern of the next few days followed the first. Work in the relative cool of the morning, a light lunch followed by a siesta until the temperature dropped, then more hours trying to give some order to the wealth of information Gavin had gathered over the last few months, followed by dinner with the rest of the group.

Eloise and Pierre, she learned, spent their days in the canopy—taking photographs and studying a particular species of wasp respectively. Lars too spent his days on a platform in the canopy forty or fifty metres above the ground, his study fruit bats. Hans, as an entomologist, seemed to have no set pattern to his whereabouts. Sometimes he was around, other times not.

Of García Montada there was never any sign, and so far Chrissy had been unable to pluck up the courage to bring his name to her lips. She waited like a cat at a mouse-hole for any mention of him, but talk was exclusively shop-talk.

She had managed to engineer a palm fan and made one for Hans too. When Lars looked left out she made a third, and after dinner the three of them would sit out in the dark with just an oil lamp shedding its glow, and listen to the sounds of the forest. Sometimes there would only be the creak of three bamboo rockers and the idle swish, swish of the fans. Always, though, there was the backdrop of the jungle—night screams, howls, cries, the dry cough of some nocturnal creature, clicks and whirrs of a thousand different species.

'What a treasure trove out there,' murmured Hans one night. 'Do you realise, Chrissy, there are more than forty thousand different species of insect in a single hectare of rain forest?'

Lars spoke. 'And over one thousand seven hundred different kinds of bird?'

Chrissy pondered for a moment. 'In one respect I'm lucky,' she said, 'depending on how you see it. There are only about a hundred different kinds of tree!'

'Not much to keep you busy!' Lars laughed.

Chrissy looked thoughtful. 'I know I'm only supposed to be here to tidy up Gavin's work—but I'm sure I can soon get most of it done.' She shot a glance at Hans to see if he got her drift.

'You want to add to it?'

She sighed. 'I'm sure he hasn't been able to record every single species in his garden——' 'Gavin's Garden' was how she jokingly referred to the hectare of forest Gavin had squared off for study. Each tree was mapped on graph paper. It was obvious there would be omissions.

'You want to go up into the canopy and have a look round for yourself?'

She nodded. 'I don't see why not. I can't stay in the lab all the time. Otherwise I might as well never have left England!'

Hans looked across at Lars. 'She can come with us in a day or two. When she sees how we have to climb up into the canopy, maybe she'll think twice!'

Chrissy shook her head. 'I know it's not easy—and it's a long way to fall. But I really want to do it. I think

I have to. It's all very well staying on the ground, but these forest trees all look the same from down here—the same smooth bark, the same identical spear-shaped leaves. It's only the flowers that reveal the existence of different species. And the flowers only grow fifty metres up!'

It was true and both men knew it. If they hadn't agreed to show her how to climb up she would have had to find out for herself.

'I knew a botanist,' said Hans, 'who trained a monkey to go up and throw down the flowers for him.'

'I don't think I've time for that,' said Chrissy with a grin.

'I only hope you've a head for heights.'

Eloise called to Chrissy as she left the house next morning. 'I'm at home today. Do you want to come in and see our humble abode?'

Chrissy ducked her head under the doorway of the bamboo hut and stepped inside. It was lighter than she'd expected, but deliciously cool even with the sun beating down on it. The sticks of bamboo were tied together with a special knot to keep each one in place, forming a wall, and it had a palm thatch resting on two cross-beams of heavier wood, which in turn rested in notches in a frame of four uprights and a centre pole.

There was a wide sleeping-platform at one end, and a few clothes hung from the central support. Apart from that there was little else. Toilet things, toothbrushes and a few odds and ends of make-up, were lined up neatly on a shelf of bamboo tied with twine to the upright that made the wall. It was all very neat, very functional. Chrissy admired the golden light that filtered in. She thought how romantic it was for the couple to start their married life in such surroundings.

'Like living on paradise isle!' she said.

'Would that it were! I'd love a dip in an ice-blue sea right now. That grey-brown soup that passes for a river out there is a real torment.'

For some reason her words made Chrissy think of García Montada. Ice-blue. Torment.

She sat down on the sleeping-platform while Eloise played hostess and offered her a drink from a small cool-box. When they had talked about this and that for a few minutes, Chrissy casually mentioned the subject of her constant thoughts, admitting only that she had met him a few days ago.

'He's not around much. I've only met him a couple of times myself,' Eloise told her. 'He checks things out now and then. Comes in to see we're not running the servants ragged, I expect—as if we would,' she added.

'What's it got to do with him?' quizzed Chrissy.

'He pays their wages, I guess.'

'He does?'

Eloise shrugged. 'Why are you so surprised?' She lifted her head and gave Chrissy an elfin grin. 'Are you as intrigued by *El Senhor* as I am? He's quite——' she paused '—how to say it? Formidable?' She burst into peals of laughter. *'Oui, oui—très formidable, un bel homme, oui?'*

Chrissy felt her face flood with colour. 'He's married, isn't he?' she said, remembering the ring he wore. 'He's also the most horrible, arrogant monster I've ever had the misfortune to come across.'

'Yes, yes, but apart from all that there is no arguing—*un très bel homme*. Were I not mad about my Pierre——' Eloise gave a very Gallic shake of the hand to demonstrate exactly what she thought of García Montada. 'A man of mystery, too, eh?' She growled deep in her throat and Chrissy couldn't help but laugh.

'I guess you've said all there is to say on that subject!'
She got up. 'Come over and have a chat in the lab later
on if you like. I've still got a lot of Gavin's stuff to do.'

'I'll come and wake you up from your dreams of
Rodrigo García Montada! But promise not to be angry.'

Smiling, Chrissy made her way across the compound
to the privacy of the lab. She didn't feel like smiling. It
was pure reflex. The formidable García Montada.
Rodrigo? Very romantic, she mocked. Pity he wasn't her
type. On the other hand, she thought as she settled to
her work, it was probably a very good job—he wore a
gold ring and, obviously the philandering type, was
hedged with every red warning sign imaginable. All
they'd shared was a kiss, that was all. An aberration.
The fact that she'd let it dominate her life for the last
few days said more about her than about him! She was
a little lonely, that was the trouble. Lonely and very
inexperienced. But there was work to do and no time
for dangerous fantasies. If Eloise was right, and he rarely
visited the compound, the chances were she would
probably never see him again.

In fact, a week passed. Hans and Lars took her to where
Lars began his daily work—the foot of a sixty metre
giant of the forest from whose branches hung a purple
climbing-rope. Looking up, Chrissy saw that it was
fastened to the first large branch, fifty feet above her
head, and then it went up—and, she knew, up and up,
dwindling far away into the dense green foliage above
her head. She stifled a shudder.

'Will you show me what you do?' she asked Lars.

He pulled at two metal hand-grips attached to the rope
and showed her how they could slide upwards, but how
a ratchet prevented them from sliding down. He put his
feet into a pair of webbing straps and demonstrated how
to edge the hand-grip upwards with all his weight in one

stirrup then, putting his weight in the other side, he managed to hoist up the other side another few inches. Slowly he began to ascend the tree. It seemed to take an age.

'And he's an expert,' murmured Hans, watching her face.

'I've still got to give it a try,' she told him. 'Otherwise how else can I get into the canopy where the blossoms are?'

'I'll help you fire a rope up. Come and show me where you want it.'

Chrissy had already studied Gavin's plan and worked out the best place to ascend. 'He seems to have covered this area pretty thoroughly,' she told Hans when he came back to the lab with her to get the necessary equipment. She indicated a square on the graph paper. He leaned over her shoulder. He was still leaning over it when the door flew open and Chrissy turned to find herself being pierced by a glance of pure ice.

'Busy?'

'Senhor...' Hans looked flustered as he went over to shake the taller man by the hand. He glanced over his shoulder at Chrissy. 'I believe you've met already?'

Chrissy couldn't bring herself to reply. All the sensible thoughts of the last few days flew out of the window. It seemed as if everything she thought important was made into nothing by his mere reappearance.

Hans was gabbling on about helping Chrissy climb into the canopy, and he was already going over to the rope, the thin one that would be shot up over the first branch by which the far stronger climbing-rope would be hauled into the tree. But Montada stopped him.

'I cannot allow it,' he said shortly. 'Surely you are not serious?' He glanced from one to the other as if amazed.

'But——' began Hans, then broke off and shot an apologetic glance at Chrissy, 'Well, maybe we should rethink...?'

Chrissy found herself trembling from head to foot. Whether with rage, irrational desire, or a mixture of the two she couldn't tell. She stood where she was, fists clenched, and asked coldly, 'I'm rather confused—does Senhor Montada have some special power I'm unaware of? I mean, in respect of the work of we foreign researchers?'

Hans gave an apologetic cough as if an underling had made an unfortunate gaffe. Montada himself smiled thinly. 'Yes, I remember our meeting in this very lab on your first morning here. If you recall I did suggest you came over to the house for a little orientation?' His expression was glacial. 'However, I'm sure Hans here will put you in the picture.' He gave Hans a cool glance. 'I know I can trust you not to allow Miss Baker to do anything foolish. I do not wish to have a hospital case, or worse, on my conscience.'

With that he went out and Chrissy could see him marching briskly across the compound towards the house. He must be going to pay the servants, she thought. And that must make him feel he could lay down the law to everyone. Well, he didn't pay *her* wages. She was a free agent. Or as free as working for the research unit in England allowed.

'Well,' she said briskly. 'Pity about all that. Now, what am I supposed to do with this rope?' She picked up the thin coil and hooked it over one arm.

Hans looked at her with reproach in his eyes. 'No, Chrissy, I'm sorry—if he gives it his veto I'm afraid that's that.'

'What?' She gazed at him in astonishment. 'Are you scared of him or what?'

Hans lifted his shoulders and let them fall. 'Yes, possibly. I wouldn't like to get on his wrong side. But it is more than that.'

'More? But why the hell should he call the shots? I don't understand!'

'He calls the shots because he owns the shots—what I mean is, he owns this——' Hans gestured round the lab.

'But I understood it was a jointly funded venture existing on grants and donations made by the participating countries——' burst out Chrissy.

'Yes, some of it. Our salaries. But not——' he paused, '—not all the rest.'

'What rest? What else is there? A wooden house, a cook and odd-job man, a couple of palm-thatched huts? It's worth a couple of thousand at most——' She was furious now.

'You don't understand. He owns—well, he owns everything.'

'What else is there except the damn forest? You'll be saying he owns that next!' she exclaimed. Then her jaw sagged.

'Yes.' Hans was still apologetic. 'Exactly my meaning. He does. He owns countless hectares of the forest. Look to the horizon in every direction—all his. I doubt whether even he knows the exact extent in figures. We are entirely beholden to him. He can order us off at any time. It is only by his magnanimity that we are allowed here at all.'

'By the grace of God himself you mean,' fumed Chrissy, unable to take it in. 'He *can't* own it—I mean——' She stomped over to the window and looked out at the endless miles of forest stretching to the horizon and beyond. Although her words denied it, she knew in her heart it was true.

It had to be.

Only a man as formidable as Rodrigo García Montada would take it on himself to lay claim to such a large slice of God's heaven.

CHAPTER FOUR

CHRISSY knew it was hopeless but she had to do it. She said, 'I'll go across and try to reason with Senhor Montada...I'm not going to take this lying down.'

With a warning not to get herself into trouble ringing in her ears, she left the lab and made her way through the dizzying heat towards the house. She forced herself to pause in the shade of the steps before going inside. What was she to say to him that would make him change his mind? She didn't know the man. She had no idea what sort of argument—if any—would sway him. Was he as autocratic as he seemed? There was only one way to find out.

Steeling herself, she made her way up the steps into the entrance. First she poked her head round the kitchen door. Senhora Suarez was busy slicing vegetables into a big cast-iron cooking-pot. 'Do you happen to know where Senhor Montada is?' asked Chrissy in a determined voice.

'He is attending to some business in his rooms, I do believe,' replied Senhora Suarez, gesturing towards the corridor.

Chrissy turned. What was he doing with rooms here? Perhaps he used the place as a kind of lodge when his royal progress brought him in this direction!

There were five doors to choose from. Two on each side of the corridor and one at the far end of it. Remembering that Lars and Hans always stepped from the veranda through the two sets of doors on the left giving on to the back of the house, she guessed that *'El Senhor'* would have the ones at the front. Naturally.

She knocked rather tentatively on the first of these and waited. Nothing happened. Deciding that she'd better try the next one, and perhaps knock a little louder, she moved further along. There was still no reply even though the sound was loud enough to rouse anybody.

Just about to apply her knuckles to the door yet again she was startled by the sound of a voice from the far end of the corridor. Pivoting, she saw García Montada leaning casually against the door-post. He must have opened the door without a sound. She wondered how long he'd been standing there, watching her nervous approach, mocking her mounting impatience at getting no response.

'You wanted me?' he asked in that seductive drawl of his.

There was no way such a simple question coming from his lips could sound innocent. She flushed, unable to stop herself. Wildly she wondered what would happen if she nodded and said, Yes, I *want* you, García Montada! She fixed her glance at a point on the door-jamb beside his left ear. 'I would like to discuss this matter with you,' she said as evenly as she could.

'Matter?' He brought a frown to his face that did nothing to mar his good looks. 'What matter?' he insisted, eyes blank.

You damn well know which matter, she wanted to spit, but, proud of her control, she replied quietly, 'The matter of my continuing Gavin's research.'

'If those are your instructions from England, to continue your predecessor's research, then——' he shrugged the broad shoulders, encased in a stiff white shirt '—only you know what you must do.'

'I agree,' she said. Stepping forward a pace so she didn't have to raise her voice, she added, 'But I can't

continue in the same way unless I can work in the canopy——'

He gave a rough gesture with one hand. 'It's crazy.
Forget it. I've already told you what I think.'

'But——'

'No buts. I've spoken.' He turned his head as if to go
back inside his room.

'I understand from Hans Bergdorf that you own the
forest,' she blurted, moving after him. 'I'm fully in-
sured. You would be in no way liable if I had an
accident... If that's the problem,' she added lamely.

'Good. But the answer is still no.'

'But why?' She was standing next to him now and the
carefully repressed attraction flared again as she came
too close. For a moment she felt winded, then the
paralysis crept into her throat and all she could do was
stare up at him, praying that the longing and the dislike,
that fiery, untameable mixture of emotions she felt, was
thoroughly masked.

He stepped back. 'Come inside.' He moved to open
the door to let her through.

With a feeling that she should by now be saying no
and fleeing for safety, she found herself entering the
lion's den.

'Take a seat,' murmured a voice directly behind her.

She was dazzled by the lightness of the room, even
though rattan blinds clacked at every window. The room
was all windows, each one shaded, and there was polished wood everywhere, and sunlight, and woven rugs,
and bright Indian hangings on the wall. It had an air of
greater comfort than she had expected, with white wicker
chairs scattered around and, she noticed, a colourful rope
hammock across one corner. There was also a rifle
propped prominently against a chair and a knee-high
rattan table with a glass of something long and cool and
green on it.

He followed her glance. She was startled when he went to the door and opened it again. She heard him call for Senhora Suarez and a sentence or two were exchanged. When he returned he was carrying a similar drink. Chrissy was standing by the window trying to prepare herself for anything.

'Don't you want to sit down?' he snapped. He gestured impatiently to one of the chairs.

Warily she placed herself on the very edge of it. He pushed the glass across the table towards her and settled back among a pile of white hopsack cushions. Designed to enhance his tan, she thought grudgingly. And they did. She sipped her drink, wondering whether she could control the wild horses galloping through her veins and whether to wait for him to begin or whether to plunge in first. But he knifed through her indecision.

'I'm not being unreasonable,' he announced, coming straight to the point. 'What you're proposing is a very dangerous thing. Tell me why you feel you need to do it.'

'I've already mentioned that,' she began, wondering what the point of all this was if his mind was already made up. 'Gavin only had time to cover one small area of the grid. I would feel my time was wasted if I didn't try to cover a little more.'

'Were you instructed to go ahead in this way?'

She dropped her glance, the lie almost begging to be told. But she couldn't say it. 'I'm sure if anyone had thought about it they would have instructed me in that way.' There was only Cavendish to veto it. Now she thought about it she knew another reason she wanted to go ahead was to prove she was somebody to be reckoned with.

'My career is very important to me,' she said, raising her glance. 'I really need to make a strong contribution.

I know I can, given the chance.' Then she bit her lip. Was this the wrong approach to a man like him?

'Ambitious and career-minded is not how I see you, Miss Baker.'

'I'm sorry to disappoint you.'

He smiled thinly. 'Have you done this sort of thing before?'

Layers of hidden meaning seemed to be hinted at in the way he was watching her. Done what? she wanted to ask. Played cat-and-mouse with the most handsome, philandering male in the entire universe? She gave him a level glance. 'I've done some climbing. I'm not a complete incompetent.'

He gave the thin smile again, but his eyes had lightened and he was thinking something else now. 'Do you imagine I'm saying "no" out of a sense of old-fashioned chivalry, perhaps?'

'You?' The exclamation was out before she could hide her astonishment.

He frowned. 'You don't see me as chivalrous?' His head tilted.

'It depends,' she replied carefully, 'on what you mean by chivalry.'

He laughed. 'Yes, maybe our understandings are too far apart. How could we be expected to understand each other when we come from opposite sides of the world?' Then he gave her a charming smile. 'My mother was English so I know the problems.'

Thus the blue eyes, she registered, wanting him to go on. His voice was like honey. If he was setting out to hypnotise her with its lilting sonorities he was winning. It was a walk-over. Mentally she gave herself a shake. 'Then you do understand how I feel?' she suggested.

He shook his head. 'Far from it. Besides, I have never lived in your country. I don't know how things go on there. My knowledge comes down to a couple of

European tours long ago.' He was frowning again and Chrissy was finding it difficult to keep up with his mercurial moods. 'I don't begin to understand what you are doing out here, so far from your own people, from young men of your own kind who would be likely to want to marry you.'

'Excuse me,' she butted in, 'I don't see marriage as the be-all and end-all of my life.'

'But you can't leave it too late.'

'I'm only twenty-three,' she pointed out. 'Time enough to think of marriage when I've established myself in a career.' No way was she going to make the same mistake as her mother—to marry before completing her training and run the risk of being left without a husband, without a job and with a child to support. But she wasn't going to tell him that. Her private affairs were none of his business.

'And you think you will still be marriageable in a few years when you decide the time is then right for you?'

Somehow he made it seem very cold-blooded. Chrissy shrugged. 'I shall have to cross that bridge when I get to it.' He was making her prickly, probing into her life as if he had a right to. 'Personally I don't believe in one rule for men and one for women. If it's not expected that a man will marry until he's got himself started in a career, why shouldn't it be the same for a woman?'

'But life is not even-handed in this respect,' he came back. 'Men don't have to be handsome in order to acquire a wife. They only need to be wealthy—or lucky.' He smiled confidently. 'Sad as it is, women lose their looks. How then will they find the husband?'

She frowned. 'I would hate to be married merely for my appearance. What sort of marriage would *that* be? Heavens! I should expect to be loved for *myself*, not for any decorative value I had!'

'What a romantic point of view. Marriage as an expression of *love*!' He was scowling, and added roughly, 'And of course, you take your looks for granted anyway, perhaps not realising that life is easy for a young woman who looks the way you do. You have the world at your feet. Now. But later things will inevitably change. Beauty does not last forever.'

Chrissy couldn't help smiling. 'How quaint!' she said before she could stop herself. 'I would have thought you'd disproved your own argument! Here I am——' she spread her arms as if offering herself, '—and I'm not able to get what I want—despite the so-called advantage of my looks!' She'd meant it half jokingly for his argument was ridiculous, but his reaction was astonishing.

He jerked back as if she'd struck him again. Uncoiling from his position in the chair opposite, he strode rapidly across the room before coming to an abrupt halt. When he swung to face her he had recovered from his brief loss of composure, but Chrissy's mind boggled at what had forced him to jerk to his feet like that.

He confirmed her suspicions when he ground out, 'Of course, you mean this foolish desire to work in the canopy like the men. I misunderstood. That is *all* you want from me?'

'What else?' she exclaimed, beetroot-faced at the impression she had unwittingly created. Not that she blamed him after that last meeting for thinking she was simply waiting for an invitation to climb into his bed! She pretended to fiddle with her glass to hide her scarlet cheeks... He was impossible. The whole situation was more than she could handle. How on earth could she get everything back on an even keel? They would never reach agreement. There were misunderstandings at every turn. It was like picking one's way across a field of thistles.

She got up. It was a waste of time. And she mustn't linger or she would only add fuel to his suspicion that she was intent on notching him up, in that distasteful phrase he had used the second time they'd met.

'Where are you going?'

She was already halfway to the door.

'Plainly you didn't invite me in so we could have a serious discussion about my request.' Her hand was already resting on the door knob.

'Come back.' It was an order.

She hesitated.

'I'm not used to having to say everything twice,' he snarled with a sudden loss of his earlier politeness. 'What's this obsession with speed? I haven't said all I want to say yet.'

The first time they'd met he'd complained they weren't being speedy enough! Controlling her urge to point this out to him, she said, 'I really don't think——'

'Sit down and listen.'

'I——'

'Damn well do it!' He moved towards her.

When she automatically flinched he growled on a different note, 'Why the hell do you bring out the worst in me? *Please*——' he put out a hand and made a small bow '—please sit down.'

When she was in the chair again, he told her, 'You have much to learn about our ways here. We take time to arrive at decisions. There is no need for mad haste, rushing hither and thither, you know. There is time enough. Time to enjoy...'

She stiffened, almost lulled until the final word into thinking he was about to take her request seriously. She tensed, waiting for what would come next. Men were the same the world over, she was thinking. This one just happened to look like a blue-eyed *conquistador*.

'Now, tell me,' he leaned back elegantly in the rattan chair. 'Why can you not let someone go up and collect your specimens for you? Tell me.'

Chrissy did a double-take. 'I hadn't thought of that. I mean, who could do it? I can hardly ask any of the others. It wouldn't be professional. They have their own research, and—and I'd quite like to do it myself actually.'

'We can't always do what we would like to do in this world, Miss Baker.'

Wondering by what small thing he had recently found himself thwarted, she frowned.

'And any more reasons?' he persisted.

She bit her lip. 'I—can't think of anything just now,' she admitted.

'Then leave it with me. Now, please, you may leave.' He got up and went over to a desk pushed into a corner. Taking it as a rather curt and unexpected dismissal, she made her way towards the door. As she reached it she felt him suddenly close behind her.

'I'm so sorry, allow me,' he murmured. Obviously pulling out all the stops to restore his image as one of society's knights in shining armour, he opened the door for her and offered a token inclination of his head as she went out. Only when she heard the door close behind her did she release some of the tension he had aroused. Running down the steps, she lifted her face to the sun for a long moment and let all the tightness drain from her body. She hadn't understood him at all this time. Instead of getting to know him better she now felt she knew him less than ever.

The feeling of knowing every single thing about him she had experienced on that first meeting in the clearing on the way here had been a complete illusion. She knew nothing. He was, as Eloise had jokingly said, a man of mystery. Why the continual about-faces, the efforts to be seen as a benign dictator rather than the tyrant he undoubtedly was? He wasn't the type to care a damn what anybody thought of him. Of that at least she was sure!

But did it matter if she couldn't find answers to the enigma? He had seemed to be amicably disposed towards her request—but *how*, she angrily registered, had she, a *free agent*, been persuaded to think of her intention to work in the canopy as a *request*? However, he had at least come part of the way to meet her. It must be a victory of sorts.

Returning to the lab, she wasn't surprised to find Hans already gone. Worried about job security, she thought bitterly. It made cowards of people if they weren't careful. Wondering how far she would go in ever risking her own job, she picked up the ropes that had been left out and toyed with them for a moment or two. She knew in theory what to do with them. Whether she would be a good enough shot to be able to get them over the right branch for an ascent was another matter. If necessary she would definitely have to have a try.

After lunch she was just settling back in the lab, having lost too much time that morning and intending to make it up despite the afternoon steam bath, when there was a loud rat-tat on the door. Puzzled, she went to open it.

'Ah, so here you are, Miss Baker. Profound apologies for the interruption.' It was García Montada at his most suave—but was there a gleam of amusement in the sky-blue depths? Before she could decide, he turned to the teenage boy lurking behind him. 'Here is Tomas. He has kindly offered to assist you.' With a sardonic smile García Montada inclined his head and swivelled to leave.

The boy looked at Chrissy and Chrissy looked at the boy. She wondered how much his "offer" had come down to a simple question of obeying orders. She gave him a smile, as if to dissociate herself from anything

García Montada might have said, and held out a hand. 'Hi, I'm Chrissy,' she announced. 'Did *"El Senhor"*——' her lip curled, '—tell you what I want?' The boy nodded. He didn't look like a boy ordered to climb to the top of a sixty metre tree against his wishes. In fact he looked positively eager to get going.

Chrissy fetched the ropes and the rest of the gear. It was quite a turn-up for the books—not only had *'El Senhor'* kept his word, he had done it in double-quick time as well! Even so, after one or two ascents Tomas might feel like a rest while she went up to have a look round for herself!

That evening Eloise and Pierre were absent because they were down-river with Pedro, Lars was feeling the heat and was lying down, and Hans, after half an hour, went off to his room to make a few observations on the latest addition to his beetle collection. That left Chrissy and Rodrigo García Montada alone on the veranda, with the cries of the night creatures filling the velvety darkness beyond the perimeter of the amber glow shed by the oil lamp above their heads.

Chrissy racked her brain for some excuse to leave too but could think of nothing, having announced at dinner that she was finished for the day and well on schedule.

She had avoided addressing García Montada just as he had seemed to avoid addressing her. Now there was silence between them, though by no means an empty one.

Eventually she felt compelled to say something to bring some normality to her jumping nerves. She searched in vain for a remark that lacked innuendo, or any suggestion of an invitation, and said at last, 'I'm surprised you're still here. I understood you visited the house only rarely.'

'You mean you feel I've outstayed my welcome?' His face was in shadow but there was no mistaking the ironic tone.

'No, of course not——' she began but he interrupted.

'Your interest in the reasons for my being here is most flattering, Miss Baker.'

'It wasn't meant to be,' she couldn't help pointing out. 'It was simply a casual observation.' Let's get that straight at least! she thought.

'A concern at any rate that seems to form the basis for most of our conversations—if such they can be called.'

His voice was level with only a hint of an inflexion that could spell danger. Chrissy ignored it. 'No doubt you have far more fascinating conversations with the sort of decorative type of woman you say you prefer.'

'Did I say that...? Anyway, I think you're quite decorative enough,' he rejoined. 'Quite the little blonde angel of most men's more primitive fantasies.'

Floored by her inability to sort the insults from the compliments, Chrissy was silent.

'I feel I've offended you now. Is it insulting to draw attention to your——' he paused as if sifting through his vocabulary for a suitable word '—to your beauty?'

'I find it offensive when men dwell on my appearance,' she said tightly. 'There's more to me than that!' Memories of what it had been like to be the accidental winner of a beauty contest came back to taunt her. 'Sometimes I feel I should try to make myself look as ugly as possible in order to be taken seriously as a human being,' she said.

'*Could* you?'

'What?' She lifted her head. His face was still in shadow but she could see the silver-blue of his eyes gleaming ferally in the darkness.

'Make yourself look ugly?' He laughed and answered his own question. 'No, I doubt it. Even first thing in the morning when most of us are at our worst you will be quite ravishing, I'm sure.'

She wondered what he would look like at his 'worst'—quite ravishing too, she thought, or the masculine, *very* masculine, equivalent. She turned away and wished he would leave. But he went on sitting there, jangling her nerves and making her wonder why it was impossible to get up and simply walk away.

'Miss Baker...' He said her name as if experimenting with it, tasting it on his lips. 'Do you prefer to be addressed thus?'

She pursed her lips. 'It's really up to you. You're the—what do they call you—*the Senhor*?'

'The lord?'

'If you say so.'

'Or do you prefer *Seigneur*?' he chuckled wickedly. 'Unafraid I shall claim my *"droit"*—?'

'I'm sure you're too much of a gentleman even to contemplate such a thing,' she riposted.

He chuckled again. It was a sound like that made by a contented predator when the prey was firmly within its grasp. But he took her by surprise. 'You may have got the wrong impression the other day. Do you remember our brief encounter in the kitchen?' He waited until she gave a faint assent. How could she not remember? Brief encounter, he called it. Why not cataclysm? Apocalypse? 'I can assure you it was unprecedented,' he went on. 'You made a gift of yourself. No man could have resisted.'

'So that's all right, then,' she said, not bothering to hide her sarcasm.

'Your meaning?'

'No blame attaches to you even though you—even though you took advantage of me——'

'*I* took advantage of *you*?' He seemed genuinely scandalised. 'Hardly a reasonable interpretation of events. You were almost naked.'

'I had no idea anyone else was around and in that heat I couldn't bear to wear anything heavier.'

'Even so——'

'Even so I was asking for it? Is *that* what you mean?'

He smiled faintly, teeth a slash of white in the shadows. 'Were you not? Have you not as you say been "asking for it" ever since we met?'

'Certainly not!'

'Do you always look at men with blind lust in your eyes as if asking to be taken——?'

'How *dare* you?' She gripped the sides of her chair.

'Don't slap my face again. The second time I will not be so well-behaved.'

'You mean you'd strike back?'

'Something would be done. That's for sure.'

'Like what? Send me back home like a naughty girl?'

'I wasn't thinking along those lines——'

'Don't threaten me, Senhor Montada, this sort of thing is not part of my contract.'

She saw him lean back in the chair beside her own. With his head resting on the cushion his face looked like a painting, all hollows and jagged cheekbones, the straight nose and full lips asking to be admired. His eyes were closed. This way he looked provokingly handsome—and he was accusing *her* of provoking *him*!

She leaned forward, wanting only to get away.

'Don't go!' He tilted his head towards her and opened his eyes a slit.

'There's no point in continuing this.' But she hesitated.

'There is every point. We are testing each other. Learning each other.'

'I think I know you as well as I wish to,' she told him, not caring what happened if only she could escape in safety. There was such threat in everything he said, but the real threat was in the way he managed to turn the threat into seduction.

Like a fly in a spider's web her mind twisted and turned for a way out. She could find it only in attack. 'I know you're arrogant and full of prejudice. Your ideas of women are feudal.'

'You know nothing of me or my ideas, Miss Baker, and I know only a little of you and yours. Whether you wish to know more has nothing to do with it. You are here on my territory for some weeks to come. It is inescapable that our paths cross.'

'Do you take so much trouble to get to know everyone who works here?'

'I can assure you this is no trouble.'

Everything she said seemed to change when he threw it back to her. She rocked more rapidly back and forth, making the fan attached to the rocker waft her hair until it lifted.

He put out a hand. 'Slow down. You make me nervous.'

'Very likely, I must say...' She turned her head. 'Do you shoot dumb, defenceless animals with that gun of yours?'

'Sometimes.'

'I don't know how you can.'

'Are you vegetarian?'

She reluctantly shook her head. 'I don't believe in killing animals for the fun of it though.'

'And you assume I do?' He turned his hunter's eyes on her.

'No doubt,' she replied quickly. 'You own everything here. Why not do what you like, play God if it amuses you?'

'You see me as a megalomaniac?'

'Oh, I understand how easy it must be—to be like that, living here so far from civilisation,' she said, not concealing her contempt. 'You are obviously lord of all you survey.'

'Not quite all.' He looked full in her face and gave her a smile of deliberate and meaningful charm.

Her lips tightened.

'But I am offending you again and without even trying. Let's agree, shall we, Miss Baker? We are two separate people with practically nothing in common. We don't even like each other very much, it seems. But, as luck will have it, here we are, stuck in the middle of the jungle without any prospect of running away to the city and city folk and what you call civilisation for some weeks to come. Don't you think we should make the best of things?'

'We don't need to make the best of things. We don't even need to meet. You don't have to be around here, do you?'

'You are concerned again with the matter of my whereabouts. How interesting.'

'Only concerned in so far as I would prefer it if you were elsewhere,' she retorted, not caring how she sounded.

He gave a grunt. 'So I gather.' He got up so suddenly she started with surprise. 'I may as well wish you goodnight. We are, as you might say, flogging a dead horse?' With a jerk of his head he turned and walked rapidly along the veranda and eventually she saw him disappear round the corner to the front where, she thought with a sudden shoot of misery, he'll no doubt find the solitude he prefers.

She had almost engineered his departure. Now he had gone. She had never spoken to anyone like that before. It was unstoppable, the feeling that came over her whenever he was around. But she was glad he had gone.

She rocked back and forth. There was nothing so lonely as the empty chair beside her. But she was *glad* it was empty. She rocked back and forth for a few minutes more. Why was it they were unable to talk to each other like two reasonable human beings? What was the point of all this sparring? Who won by it? He had kissed her by mistake the other day. She had responded with an eagerness that was out of character. They both accepted that it was best forgotten.

Still rocking quickly back and forth, she thought, What if he had intended to wipe the slate clean this evening? He had made some effort to put things on a different footing by offering the services of Tomas. So why had she made matters worse from the moment she had opened her mouth?

Another wave of misery overcame her. The night seemed full of loneliness despite the multitude of fellow creatures in the forest.

After a while she got up, letting the chair rock wildly as she moved away. No point in sitting out here alone. She would go back to her room and find a book. Glancing at the clock as she went inside, she saw it was nearly midnight. Maybe it was time to turn in. The house was as silent as a morgue. For the first time she wondered if she had been right to take this assignment. The work was fine. But she hadn't expected to encounter difficulties beyond that.

She reached her room. Unhappiness made her slow, and before going in she couldn't hold back a tear or two as she rested her forehead against the door. Remembering some of the things she had said to him, she was really appalled. He seemed to have forced them out of her against her will. Despairingly she glanced along the corridor. At the furthest end, on the opposite side of the house, she could see the door to his room.

Just as she turned away she glimpsed his athletic shape emerging from the kitchen. Casting a glance down the corridor, she knew he had seen her, but he turned towards his own room and she slipped out of sight before he reached the end.

With a leaden feeling she switched on the lamp and began to undress.

Once in bed, she pulled the mosquito netting around her and, with just the light from the lamp at the head of the bed, began to flick unseeingly through a paperback. It was useless trying to sleep feeling like this. Even with her eyes open she could see his face dancing before her. Now she really thought about it he had looked almost vulnerable with his head tilted back on the cushion, rocking gently, almost imperceptibly, to and fro. How did she know he hadn't been wounded by her remarks? But then, he had given as good as he got.

She put the book to one side. He had commented on the fact that they didn't even like each other much. Doubtless *he* felt that. She had hardly put herself out to be liked! But he provoked her so with his assumption—not an assumption—with his justifiable air of authority. How could she expect him to behave any differently when he was such a commanding figure?

In her heart of hearts she knew that liking was an irrelevance. He wasn't the sort of man to arouse lukewarm feelings. It would have to be either love or hate. Perhaps it wasn't dislike they felt then, but hate? The truth was she didn't know what she felt...except confusion. But she dared not put any other name to this hell of emotion. Now, in the silence of the night, it felt like tenderness, like longing... It felt like love. The sort that went painfully unrequited.

There was a knock on her door. Thinking it must be Eloise, back later than expected, she didn't move but called out, 'Come in.'

The door swung open. It was him. 'I saw your expression as you came in here. I couldn't go to sleep with this between us.' He came swiftly into the room and closed the door behind him. 'Am I to call you Miss Baker for the next five weeks?'

Chrissy sat upright. Naked except for a cotton sheet, she clutched wildly for it. For once he didn't appear to notice.

'Well?' he asked. 'Tell me.' He came to the edge of the bed. They were looking at each other through a haze of white net. 'You look like a bride,' he murmured. 'Chrissy? Christine? Which must it be?'

'Friends call me Chrissy...' she blurted, knowing there were tears on her cheeks but unable to wipe them off without releasing her hold on the sheet bunched beneath her chin.

He thrust the netting aside. 'Can you bring yourself to call me something other than *El Senhor*?' He stood tall and dark and powerful beside the bed as if ready to possess her.

When her eyes widened he murmured, 'Well? What about Rodrigo—Rod——' he shrugged his heavy shoulders '—whichever you prefer.'

He sat on the edge of the bed, the white netting trailing over him, and reached for her with one hand while wiping her cheeks with the fingers of the other one. 'Angel, we can't say goodnight like that. Not with something like that between us. Never like that.'

As his arms circled her, holding her carefully against his broad chest, her senses became alert. Everything became a hundred times more vivid—from the distant cries out in the forest to the pungent vanilla scent of his skin, the hard shape of his muscles against her burning skin, and the tiny lines in the corners of his eyes. Her hands automatically met behind his back.

She had never felt so close to anyone. She could see the black, glossy raven-wing of his hair against her cheek and measure the wild pulsing in his neck at the side of her mouth.

It was all new, holding a man like this, being held by a man, by this man, this special man, who held her with such tenderness. It was like entering a world that had been lying in wait just over the threshold from ordinary life—she felt more alive than at any other time in her entire life. It was so magically new. He was her new-found land.

CHAPTER FIVE

'EYES of emerald, hair of gold, skin of pearl...' Rodrigo ran a finger experimentally over Chrissy's shoulder, making her shiver with anticipation until the clamouring of common sense began to scream a long drawn-out 'no' in her head.

He was trembling with suppressed emotion and she could feel the tension building inside him. But she was helpless to do anything about it. Soon it would break down his defences and her own would crumble at the same instant. He had come to her when she was at her weakest, feeling lost and vulnerable. Now all she could do was gaze trustingly into his silver-cobalt eyes, waiting for him to take her fate in his hands.

But he was waging a battle against fate too. He didn't kiss her. She heard him give a sharp groan as he pressed his mouth feverishly against her hair, then, with a reluctant thrusting of his hands, he released her.

He got up, the mosquito netting swishing back into place until all she could see was his dark shape looming in the shadows on the other side. His expression was difficult to discern.

'I didn't mean to hurt you this evening,' he told her in a voice that was strangely level. 'There are too many barriers between us so we should not be surprised there are misunderstandings.' He seemed to incline his head. 'We are friends again?'

He took her silence for assent. She sat upright with the sheet wrapped round her waist where it had fallen in the suddenness of his embrace. Then he went out.

74

Friends? She was aghast. How could he use such a word with this wildness between them? Then she remembered the ring with the crest on it. Did it really mean he was married? She didn't know. There had been no mention of a wife and he didn't have the air of being tied to anyone.

She lay back on the pillow. Whether he was married or not, she had to stop feeling like this—it was too dangerous. *He* was too dangerous. He was too handsome, too powerful, too—too sexually lethal. He was more of everything that spelt bewitchment than any man she had ever imagined.

Then she wondered why he had bothered to come to her room. He seemed to have the idea of putting things right between them. But now she felt worse than ever. What was she to make of him? How should she be when he blew both hot and cold? At the beginning she thought he disliked her as much as she first thought she disliked him—yet her own feelings had changed, and his passionate embrace just now seemed to show they were both being driven by the same lethal attraction.

Next morning she missed seeing him at breakfast, though she knew he was still around. Instead of lingering at the house she spent the morning with Tomas gathering specimens from the canopy—she standing patiently at the bottom of the ascent tree while he carefully brought a profusion of blooms to her. The huge waxy flowers were mainly unidentifiable, only a few of them already recorded in Gavin's notes. She was pleased with their haul and decided to get to work on them straight away in the relative coolness of the lab. They were easily sorted into two groups—the scarlet nectar-filled ones attracting insects and small mammals and the others, pale in colour, that attracted fruit bats by their rank odour.

Curling her nose, she made two trips to the lab,
carrying the pale bunch of orchid-type varieties at arm's
length and wondering if she would be able to put up
with the foetid odour for long. Inside, she opened a
window at the far end of the lab, placing them in jars
of water and deciding to deal with them first. She ranged
the poinsettia-types near her work-bench where she could
breathe in their sweet perfume as she prepared drawings.

Tomas went back to the kitchen. He was a nephew of
Senhora Suarez, she had gathered, but how he had turned
up at so opportune a moment to have this job alotted
to him she hadn't been able to find out.

She worked steadily for the rest of the morning. Every
time a stray thought about Rodrigo—Rod—careered into
her mind, she methodically repressed it. It was no good
allowing herself to start out on the path if she wasn't
going to complete the journey—what she eventually
wanted was marriage and children and true love. Giving
in to her turbulent feelings for Rod would leave her
broken. He was out of bounds. It was best to stop now
before it was too late. Fortunately he seemed to feel the
same way. His abrupt exit last night after he had prof-
fered that near-apology showed that he wanted to keep
her at arm's length too; because of the dislike he claimed
to feel and also because he was perhaps more faithful
than she had imagined to the woman for whom he wore
the gold wedding band.

It was as if she had been offered the keys of paradise
only to have them snatched away again.

Lunch was a solitary affair on the veranda at the back.
Senhora Suarez and Chrissy chatted for a few moments,
and with the extra help of hand gestures Chrissy managed
to glean the fact that Eloise and Pierre were staying at
the small town down-river where the paddle-boats
docked, but she couldn't understand what had given rise
to this change of plan. Hans and Lars were both off

again on their separate trails. And as for anyone else—
she was training herself to avoid his name—there was
the usual mysterious absence.

As she got up to go Senhora Suarez returned. '*El
Senhor* has a message for you.' Seeing the housekeeper
gesture towards the far end of the corridor, Chrissy
guessed she was supposed to go to his lair. So he had
been there all through lunch. Fair enough. So they were
avoiding each other! But she still approached his room
with caution.

He was sitting at the desk with his feet stretched out
on a corner, immersed in a conversation in Portuguese
on his mobile phone.

He indicated a chair when she came in and she waited
reluctantly for him to finish so they could get it over.
Message? she wondered. She hoped things were all right
at home.

'Your two colleagues have decided not to return. Some
mild complication.' He turned to look at her. 'Madame
Martin asks would you pack their few belongings from
their quarters? I will have someone send them on.' He
turned back to the phone and began to dial again.

'Is that all?' At least it wasn't bad news from home.
But she was slightly taken aback by his abrupt manner.

His head turned sharply to look at her. 'All? Yes. Can
you manage it?'

'I expect so.' She rose, and even as she went out he
was talking rapidly to someone on the other end of the
line.

Thinking there was no time like the present, she went
outside and crossed the blazing yellow stretch of earth
between the main house and the palm huts. She would
gather the Martins' things together right away. Today
the bamboo hut seemed alive with the whirr of insects
and the continual rustling of the wind in the palm-leaf

thatch. As before it glowed inside with the soft orange of filtered sunlight.

There was precious little to get together. Eloise seemed to have taken the make-up with her. One or two shirts and blouses drooped on hangers on the central pole and there was a battered-looking pair of boots hanging by their laces from a spar. She was just about to take them down when the door rustled open and Rodrigo entered.

'Be careful,' he warned. 'The jungle reclaims everything as soon as it can. Already you may find unexpected creatures inhabiting the corners.' He came over and up-ended one of the boots. A lizard dropped out and ran across the earth floor. 'See? Luckily not a poisonous kind.' He looked down at her. 'I should have warned you but I was preoccupied when you came in. My managers are having problems with one of the fruit crops. I'm going back up-country at once. Will you promise to be careful?'

Chrissy bit her lip and nodded. 'There isn't much to do anyway.' The air seemed buzzingly alive, vibrating with a wealth of life in which they seemed a tiny part. She found it impossible to tear her glance from his. Strips of yellow sunlight painted his face but his eyes were as clear and endless as the sky itself.

He raised one hand and brushed her hair with his fingertips. There was a moment when they hovered on the brink of something else but he said quickly, 'I don't usually spend so much time here. When I leave I shall stay up at the hacienda. By the time I return you'll be in Europe.'

She nodded. There was an air of completion about the way he spoke. He was telling her that, whatever world they had hovered near, the gates were now closed. That was how it had to be. She was relieved they were in agreement on one thing at least and that there were going to be no problems—other than the one of schooling her

heart to forget that overwhelming sense of home-coming
when he held her in his arms last night.

When he went out she stood for several moments, just
staring at the space he had occupied, and wondering if
it was love, this painful, breath-tightening hunger—or
whether it owed more to anger. She couldn't forget the
things he had said and done that had rankled. Only
later—back to that kiss, back to the embrace—had he
begun to appear in a different light.

Angry with herself for mooning over him like this, she
quickly gathered all the contents of the hut together, even
to the extent of stripping the sheets off the bed, and
carried the whole lot back to the house. He must have
left already, she thought when she saw the door at the
far end wide open and Senhora Suarez busy with a
sweeping brush within. She piled everything neatly in
the kitchen and went to let her know what she had done.

Once outside again she walked blindly back towards
the forest. There was no point in going into the lab. It
was too hot to work and even though it was humid under
the trees there was enough happening to keep her mind
occupied inside safe boundaries. She reached the ascent
tree and gazed up the massive trunk towards the scaf-
folding of boughs from one of which the scarlet climbing-
rope was dangling. Having watched Tomas ascend as
well as having that first demonstration from Lars, she
knew exactly how to go about the business of climbing
up.

Feeling the sort of recklessness that came from the
pangs of unrequited yearning, she decided she might as
well have a go. Carefully grasping the two hand-hooks,
she next placed one foot in the sling, then hung on as
the rope jerked wildly when she lifted her other foot and
put it in place. After a pause to allow the rope to settle
she pushed the hand-grip upwards, remembering at the

same time to shift her weight into one stirrup as Lars had instructed her.

Bit by bit she edged up the rope. Her shirt was dripping by the time she was half-way up. No hurry, she reminded herself, I can take my time. It was easy to rest in the stirrups until she felt ready to proceed. Then she was off again until finally, after only one more short rest, she reached the first stage.

Now sitting astride the branch as she had seen Tomas do, she made sure she was holding on tightly before she risked a glance upwards. The rope snaked up another twenty feet or so before vanishing into a mass of foliage. Up there it would be as different as could be imagined—moss and algae covering the branches in profusion. Wondering if there should be some sort of safety rope, she took a deep breath and forced herself to go on.

At last, feeling wet and hot, she reached the final stage. Now it was a question of clambering through the branches to the upper layer. With a shout of triumph she at last emerged out of the humid twilight into fresh air and sunshine.

A limitless meadow of leaves stretched all around her. The wind blew refreshingly through the crowns of the trees and here and there one or two isolated giants emerged from the dimpled canopy. As she looked around a swarm of fluff-fairies from the silk cotton trees billowed like thistledown and somewhere out of sight she could hear a troop of chattering monkeys.

There were parrots clambering about as clumsily as she was herself and countless other birds unrecognisable to her untrained eye. She could see humming-birds, though, and watched several of them hovering delicately above clumps of scarlet flowers. A monkey paused close by and drank nectar from a bell-shaped flower before swinging off after his friends.

There were one or two dangers to watch out for, she reminded herself. Tiny twig-thin snakes, the tiger cats they called margay and, worst of all the harpy, a crested eagle, a ferocious and speedy hunter. But she had seen no sign of the huge platform of twigs on which a single nestling would be raised and she reminded herself that the worrying dangers were the small things—wasps and poison tree frogs and probably a million other as yet uncollected and unnamed creatures that swung and flew and crawled in profusion within the canopy of leaves.

After collecting several interesting-looking flowers that Tomas had missed she eventually decided to face the descent. This was decidedly easier than going up, even though she had to be careful not to crush her flower collection as she slid back into the damp twilit world beneath. She reached the ground in triumph. Tomorrow she would return. Tomas could come up if he wanted, but she could easily do without him now—especially as there was going to be nobody around to stop her!

There was still nobody at the house, apart from Senhora Suarez and her husband, when she returned, and again she ate alone. When she put her concern for the two men into words Senhora Suarez shrugged graphically. 'Men!' she dismissed them all. 'Who know, eh?'

This time Chrissy did retreat to her room to read and managed most of the novel before sleep claimed her.

She was awoken early next morning by the sound of a light knock on her door. Dragging a sheet around her, she emerged from beneath the mosquito netting and opened it warily this time. But it was Hans.

He was looking worried, his freckled face unusually grim. 'Have you seen Lars in the last twenty-four hours?' he demanded without preamble.

When she shook her head he slumped against the door. 'I'm worried,' he said, confirming her impression. 'He went out yesterday morning and since then—*nichts*.'

'Anything I can do?' she asked, her worry now mirroring his own.

He shook his head. 'I know most of his beat. I'll take another look round with Suarez right now.' He was about to turn away when he gave her one of his old smiles. 'Don't worry. There's nothing you can do. You may as well continue as usual. He sometimes stays out overnight in one of the hides but he usually tells someone first.' With a lift of his hand he departed.

Wondering whether she could have done anything, she got ready to go out herself. At least she could keep her eyes open as she followed the map into the forest, though soon she took another direction and came out at the foot of the ascent tree again.

It was maybe ten o'clock and Chrissy had been happily occupied in the clear air of the topmost layer of the canopy when she heard a distant roar. At first she thought it was thunder. Storms were rare in this region— the climate varied little throughout the year and rainfall was steady and predictable. Were there storms? she wondered. But it was too regular for thunder, and besides, it seemed to be getting louder.

Then she realised it was an aircraft of some sort. She strained her neck to see which direction it was coming from. Sound seemed to ricochet around the leafy meadow in which she was sitting and it was impossible to pin-point the direction whence it came. Then suddenly there was a whooshing roar and a dark shape seemed to burst from beneath the trees, pitching and swooping like a giant eagle. She shuddered and clung more tightly to the branch she was sitting on.

It was a helicopter. All black, an alien thing in the bright green world of the rain forest, it disappeared in a glint of sun-struck metal as swiftly as a falcon stooping to its prey.

Chrissy felt disturbed after this as if the sunlit natural world had been invaded by something sinister. Unable to settle back to a serious exploration of the new species around her, she eventually made the descent clutching a few orchids and an unusual yellow trumpet-shaped flower. There was a shock waiting for her at the foot of the tree. No sooner had her feet touched ground than she heard a sound behind her and her arms were clamped painfully to her sides. Lashing out without thinking, she felt her heel connect with something hard.

The familiar scent of vanilla and the blur of a white shirt as she jerked her head back told her abruptly who held her prisoner.

'I told you not to go up there! Didn't I?' He shook her and repeated, 'Didn't I?'

They were back to the dog-fight manners of their first meetings, before the time when he had apparently decided to contest an award for chivalry.

But if it was war, she was ready. She had a lot of pent-up emotion to get off her chest. 'Take your disgusting hands off me!' she yelled in his face. 'I don't obey orders from you or from anyone else, not even if you think you rule the universe!'

He was shaking her again, nearly making her teeth rattle, his face a mask of rage, with a line of white around his lips. 'You have two choices, you little fury: either you do as I say or you go back where you came from.'

Chrissy felt suddenly betrayed. He had said he was leaving, never to return. She had suffered the pangs of bereavement for nothing. Here he was, sneaking back almost straight away. 'You do one thing and say another!' she shrieked. 'Why should I have to take notice of an arbitrary despot like you? And get your hands off!'

She began to wriggle like a wild cat, but he slammed her back against the broad base of the tree and pinned her to it by the shoulders with both hands. In order to stop her kicking him he then locked his pelvis against hers. The action only made her see red. But even as she jerked her head from side to side she could feel her strength ebbing. He could do that. Just by touching her. Yet now she saw him in his true colours her recent weakness for him had dissolved like mist. There was no way, melting touch or not, she would ever give in.

'Calm down,' he was saying over and over again, 'just calm down.'

'*Me?* You're the one! You're furious just because somebody dared to disobey you! I'd hate to be one of your servants if you treat a complete stranger like this!'

He was still murmuring soothing words to her, but he broke off to say, 'My staff seem very happy. You don't think I have to shout at them, do you?'

'If that's true why shout at me?' Then she jerked her head sideways. 'Stop it! Stop looking at me like that . . .' She darted a glance at him. 'Why don't you leave go of my shoulders and just back off?'

'I'm not sure you won't fly at me again. You have a nasty kick.'

'You deserve more than that. Scaring me out of my skin. You must have been lying in wait for me.'

'Nothing of the sort. I just happened to walk up.'

'Just happened to walk up?' Plainly he was lying. It was quite difficult to find the ascent tree if you didn't have Gavin's map in your hand.

'I'm not interested in whether you believe me or not. I'm not in the habit of lying. I came out to find you. There's been some trouble. As these things happen in threes I thought I would check you out. Now thank me for taking the trouble.'

'*Thank* you? That's the last thing I'll ever do!'

'Suit yourself. You simply show bad manners, immaturity and utter selfishness. Do you never think of anyone but yourself?' Suddenly his face took on a grimmer expression. 'Hasn't it entered your silly head that there is a good reason to bring me back here so shortly after leaving the place? I seem to remember I even told you I would definitely not be back.'

'It's because of your arbitrary nature, I suppose,' she jerked out. 'Why ask me? How should I know what goes on in your mind?' He was still pinning her against the tree and despite her hostility she could feel his hard body inflaming a traitorous desire inside her.

'Think.'

'Think?'

'Did you not see my helicopter overhead? From up there surely you saw it?'

She nodded. 'Yours? I saw a black helicopter. I didn't know it was yours.'

He seemed to think this explained things and Chrissy herself was finding it hard to keep track of what they were saying. She gave a little mewing sound in her throat as his lips seemed to swim before her eyes. Suddenly she found herself abruptly released. As she stumbled a hand came out and gripped her by the upper arm and started to drag her back through the trees.

'I have to get back to the house and you're coming with me. You can't be trusted not to get up to more tomfoolery out here. I shall seriously consider sending you back home.'

'You make me sound like a parcel,' she mocked. 'What if I won't go?'

'You will. Or you'll find yourself in deep trouble with the authorities.'

'You need officialdom to back you up, do you?' she hissed.

'Don't goad me, Chrissy. I haven't made up my mind what I'm going to do with you, but be sure of one thing: whatever I do I won't need the help of anyone else to do it!' He swung her round so strongly she bumped up against him, then his arms came round her and his hot lips were pressing rapaciously over hers. She was all flame and honey and for a split second out of time her anger spiralled out of sight. But when he released her the look of satisfaction on his face brought it swooping back. 'You see, I make no idle threat,' he told her. 'Be warned.' As if satisfied he had proved his point, he continued to drag her towards the house, despite her yelps of protest.

When they got back the reason for his initial fury was explained. Lars had spent the night in a hide within the canopy as Hans had surmised. But on climbing down that morning he had slipped and fallen from branch to branch a long way through the canopy before he had managed to get a strong enough hold on one of the algae-covered branches. He had then let himself down on the rope, when he finally managed to find it again, his progress slow and agonising because, he said, he thought he'd broken his back. He had managed to drag himself a few yards from the base of the tree when Hans had found him.

The helicopter had come in response to a call for help and now it had taken off again to take Lars and the guilt-ridden Hans to the nearest hospital.

'That's why I don't want you climbing about by yourself. There are many other dangers you are no doubt unaware of too,' he added icily. Apparently he hadn't forgiven her for the things she had said. The kiss had been a punishment.

She hated him. But she saw the reason for his anger even if she didn't agree that he had cause to worry. 'I'm not surprised he slipped if he's been perched up in a tree all night. Anyone would slip. He was probably half asleep.'

'So you are not to be trusted?'

She glared at him.

He gave a thin smile in reply. 'I suppose if you were calm enough right now you would say, "On the contrary I *am* to be trusted, I've made no promise not to go into the tree"?' When he saw her eyelids flicker in acknowledgement he added, 'At last I think I'm beginning to understand you.'

'I wouldn't get too involved in the exercise. Obviously you want me to leave.'

'Yes. True.' His lips tightened. 'I shall tell you later when you may go. And where you will be going to.'

'What?' She gazed at him in astonishment, but without answering he turned on his heel and went out.

Chrissy sat on the railing of the veranda and gazed back at the house. What did he mean by that last remark? Well, it probably didn't mean a thing. It would be strange being here without Hans and Lars and she wondered how long Hans would stay away. It was like an Agatha Christie mystery where all the suspects disappeared one by one.

She got up and went inside. She found it shocking to discover her crazy infatuation turning so suddenly to hatred again. But she should have realised that emotions which effervesced like that would come rapidly to nothing. It was lucky she hadn't surrendered to his practised Casanova charms! Now there really would have been a wailing and a gnashing of teeth!

Feeling quite perky, as if with their antagonism in the open it had cleared the air, she strolled into the sitting-room and poured herself a nice, long, drink. Then as she turned she gave a gasp. Reclining on one of the sofas was a young girl of about sixteen or seventeen. She had her eyes shut and it gave Chrissy a chance to give her a careful look.

She was exquisitely beautiful, with a pert face and long raven-black hair coiling over a tiny bosom. Gold gleamed at throat and wrists. Chrissy stepped a little closer. Then the girl stretched her left hand above her head. It was impossible not to see. She wore a thin gold ring on her wedding finger... and it bore the same crest as the one Rodrigo wore.

Feeling dizzy, Chrissy could only gape. So far she had managed to push to one side the vague questions that crested ring had aroused. Many men wore rings and usually it meant nothing. But now, seeing one with an identical eagle crest, her mind rampaged with speculation. It could surely mean only one thing.

This was the bride of García Montada.

All her carefully engineered assurances to herself collapsed in a heap of dust. Hated him, did she? So why this dreadful, wrenching sickness clawing at her insides?

She was groping for something to hold on to when he came back into the room.

'Get your things,' he ordered with a sweeping glance to encompass the two women. 'The helicopter will be here in ten minutes.' Then he turned to what Chrissy now knew to be his girl-bride. 'Come, *caro*, wake up. We have to leave.'

CHAPTER SIX

CHRISSY hadn't really believed Rodrigo was married. Or maybe she just hadn't wanted to believe it? He didn't act married. And, she defended herself, at home wedding-rings were worn on the left hand. Only in some countries they were worn on the right. His was on the left. But was that the custom of the country or not? It was just a ring. She hadn't known what it meant. Now she still didn't know—but she knew that Juanita was no figment of her imagination.

They were crammed in the four-seater helicopter, the two women at the back. Rod was sitting at the front beside the pilot and before they fastened their seatbelts Juanita was kneeling up on her seat behind him with her arms clasped round his neck, resting her black head against his, chattering and giggling and playing with his hair in a kittenish sort of way until they were ready to leave.

She must have made a joke about his hair being too long because she pulled it and turned to Chrissy, saying something in Portuguese, and Rod gave her a playful pat over his shoulder, catching Chrissy's glance as he did so. His eyes changed from laughter to something else in a moment, like a cloud covering the sun. Chrissy pretended to look out of the window. Juanita's skittishness would have been charming in any other situation. Now it was as painful as a hundred knives in her heart.

With a lurch the helicopter climbed into the air, hovered, then began its swooping journey over the tops of the trees. Despite her painful emotions Chrissy couldn't help being enthralled by the sight. At his boss's request the pilot hovered whenever there was anything of special interest to see, and Rod handed her a pair of binoculars so she could see the flora more clearly. From a distance the canopy looked like a vast cauliflower.

It was too noisy to talk and she had no idea how long they were going to be in the air but when Juanita touched her on the arm and pointed to one side she saw what she first took to be the horizontal layers of the sky—then she realised it was the distant sea. Closer, clinging to the edge of the land, was a collection of white buildings, a village perhaps. Juanita was smiling. She pointed again. This then was their destination.

As they drew near Chrissy got a better look at the buildings. They were arranged among trees and she could see a yellow road winding below with people walking on it and a man on horseback. Then the trees opened out— they were flying low now—and she saw a large white house with a shingled roof and balconies. Flower-filled patios and symmetrical gardens surrounded it like the setting for a jewel.

The yellow road went up to an arched gateway beneath which a cart piled with honey-coloured fruit was passing. The road stopped there, but they flew on over the roof of the house and across an oblong of turquoise water sheltered by an avenue of palms until they reached a meadow with a few long-legged horses in it. Then suddenly, gently, there was grass all around them and instead of looking down at a collection of toy buildings and swimming-pools everything had swung giddily back to life size.

When the engines were cut Juanita was already out of her seatbelt, her arms round Rod's neck again. He patted the back of her hand and untwined the brown arms with their gold bracelets, getting out first with a

word to the pilot as he swung to the ground. Juanita
jumped down into his arms and he spun her round before
depositing her in the grass.

Chrissy teetered in the doorway. He didn't expect her
to jump into his arms like that, did he? As if he could
read her mind he gave her a lop-sided smile as if daring
her, but she ignored it and clambered down unaided.

'Now what?' she asked when she came up beside him.

'Now we have lunch.'

She followed him across the paddock, watching him
pause for a minute to run his hands over the silken sides
of one of the horses, then the three of them moved off,
Juanita running on ahead like a little child then coming
back to swing on his arm.

He must love all that attention, thought Chrissy
miserably. They made a slightly incongruous couple
because he was so much older, sterner, and so author-
itative. But she could see that a man like him would
enjoy having someone so playful around for after hours.
She warned herself not to be bitter—it was impossible
to dislike Juanita—and followed them both into the
house.

It was really quite impressive, she thought as she
looked round. The house was cool and white inside, with
refreshing touches of green from baby palms in big pots,
the silky green of cushions and window-hangings setting
off the simplicity of white marble and stucco. Rodrigo
García Montada was obviously a wealthy man.

'Juanita,' he growled, 'show Chrissy where she can
wash—and ask Rosa which is to be her room.' He turned
to Chrissy herself. 'Juanita will bring you outside. We're
having lunch on the terrace. Don't be long. We have
much to discuss.'

'We certainly have!' she exclaimed. Since he had ac-
costed her at the foot of the tree she hadn't had a chance

to ask anything. The burning question was, how soon could she get back to work?

Juanita was leaning on the marble balustrade of a wide, shallow staircase that continued in a gallery around the main hall. When she saw Chrissy coming she waited for her and they walked up together.

'Who is Rosa?' asked Chrissy as they reached what was evidently a bathroom.

Juanita shook her head. 'How you say?' she giggled. 'No English, sorry.' She pushed open the door and ushered Chrissy inside.

I've seen smaller bathrooms, she thought as she gazed around in awe. In fact all the ones I've seen were smaller. It really had to be the biggest bathroom ever. The white marble floor made it look even more vast. There were french windows and a balcony at one end, then there was a huge sunken tub like a small swimming-pool, two showers, and a bright blue square of water that she took to be the jacuzzi. Apart from that there was a tempting array of gels and oils and perfume, enough to stock an expensive little shop.

'For guests,' said Juanita, dragging out the words with pride. 'You are guest. Here.' She turned on one of the showers. 'You have.' She suddenly put her fingers up as if she had remembered something then dashed from the room.

It wasn't towels or soap that had sent her scurrying away, thought Chrissy, looking longingly at the crystalline drops of water spraying on to the white and green tiles and then at the thick white towels folded neatly on a tiled shelf, for there were those in plenty.

Just being here made her realise how she'd been roughing it. Sitting up in the forest canopy, then being dragged here without even having time to run a comb through her hair. She glanced at the mirror down one wall and saw that she did indeed look a wreck. Her blonde hair, scraped back in a pony-tail, was straggling in wisps around her face and the old bottle-green shirt and trousers she wore were crumpled and stained from climbing about among the branches.

The door opened and Juanita came back inside carrying a bundle of bright garments. 'For you. Shower. Then yes?' She plonked the heap of clothes into Chrissy's arms. 'See you in *un momento*?' She went over to the shower, stuck her hand out as if testing the temperature, then nodded and gestured to try it.

'Why not?' She smiled her thanks and began to undress as the girl went out.

The image that greeted her in the mirror ten minutes later was a transformation. Hair washed in one of the aromatic gels and falling in damp tendrils around her shoulders, fingers and toe-nails cleaner than they had been for the last week, a whiff from one of the heavenly scented bottles and a strip of amber-coloured silk tied sarong-style over one shoulder all made her feel human again.

Her hair was almost dry as she made her way down the marble staircase. Juanita, wearing a tiny strapless sundress, came out of a side door. 'Now we eat,' she said.

Feeling a little nervous at the battle she knew lay ahead when Rodrigo started to lay down the law again, as he was bound to do, she followed the bobbing figure of his child-bride and tried to tell herself that this time next week she would probably be back in grey old England and everything that was happening now would seem like a fantastic dream.

Rodrigo was sitting on the balustrade that separated the terrace from the paved area around the pool. He was wearing a white cotton jacket, white vest that revealed a tantalising expanse of tanned muscle and chest-hair, and baggy pale grey trousers. He wouldn't have looked out of place on the front cover of a magazine. Again Chrissy recalled Eloise's words—'man of mystery'—and wondered about him. Where his wealth and his apparent leisure came from.

He was watching her as she came out under the green and white striped awning that covered the dining table, but pretended to be looking somewhere else when he saw her watching him. So it's to be cat-and-mouse again, she thought, sitting down in one of the comfortable white wooden chairs with its plump green cushion. Pretty green and white napkins fluttered on the table, and the glint of crystal, silver and fine china, with a flower display of pale roses and lavender, gave the setting a picture-book air.

The meal when it came was served by a bewildering number of dark-haired maids, but the wine was poured solemnly by a young man of around Chrissy's own age. She felt slightly ill at ease to be the recipient of such lavish attention, but it was obviously all in the day's work for the other two. Juanita chatted non-stop until Rodrigo said sharply, 'English or nothing, Juanita. You should know enough by now. How are your lessons going?'

The girl pulled a pert face. 'Very good. I speak very good.' Then she shot a mischievous glance at Chrissy. 'I speak good, yes? You tell him.'

Chrissy tried to hide a smile.

'Don't encourage her, Chrissy. She needs none of your influence.'

She wondered how he could respect a wife he had to treat like a child. 'I shall be leaving soon, so there's no danger of my being a bad influence,' she sparked back, annoyed with him as well as determined to set the record straight so there could be no misunderstandings about her eagerness to get back to work.

'I said we'll discuss that.'

'You said we'd discuss it at lunchtime.' Her eyes opened wide.

'So let's discuss it now if you insist.'

'When can I leave?'

'If you're going to take that attitude you cancel out any chance of a proper discussion,' he came back. 'You've only just arrived and now you want to go away again. Haven't you been quite well looked after so far?'

'That's not the point and you know it. I have work to do. That's why I came here in the first place. Now I've been forcibly stopped from working. It's not good enough.'

'Would you rather I'd left you at the forest house by yourself?'

'I would have been all right with Senhora Suarez and her husband around——' she bit back.

'But they are now on leave.'

'What?'

'They are taking a well-deserved six-week break.'

'Under your instructions?'

'Naturally under my instructions.'

'But why—I thought they were supposed to be running the place? Isn't anyone else taking over?'

'I really can't spare anyone.'

'There must be someone. Everybody doesn't have to wait for you to give them a job, do they?'

'They do when they live on my land.'

'Your land.' She looked down at her plate. 'It can't all be yours.'

'Everything we flew over this morning is most definitely mine. Unfortunately to find the sort of help you would need at the forest house you would have to return to the city and try one of the employment agencies. Even then you might find it difficult to persuade anyone to come out here. Away——' he smiled cruelly, mocking her own words '—from civilisation.' He went on, 'Even if you did manage to find someone I would not permit them to work on my land and in my property.'

'I could live there alone——'

'Really?' He gave a soft laugh with just a hint of menace in it. 'I must say you are a most difficult young woman. It doesn't yet seem to have occurred to you that you have no choice, emphatically no choice but to do as I say.'

'I'd like to go home,' she muttered, furious and not a little scared as the truth of what he was saying began to sink in.

'Home? Tell me about your home. I imagine it's very different from this.'

'Naturally. My mother is an ordinary woman not a medieval monarch——' She bit back the words at once but it was too late. He was laughing softly, laughing at her, as if she were a child like Juanita.

She lifted her blonde head and gave him a pitying glance. 'Have you *any* idea how other people live?'

His eyes darkened. 'Are you criticising me for happening to inherit what has been in my family for three hundred years? I didn't ask for power—it was given to me as a responsibility. Are you holding it against me?'

'Would it matter?'

Their glances meshed.

'You two, so serious!' Juanita tapped Rodrigo on the hand, 'What are you talking? I don't understand.'

'You're not alone, *caro*.' He gave her a brief smile then his glance swivelled to Chrissy again. 'I asked you about your home. I want to know about it.'

'I have a one-bedroomed flat in the university town where I work,' she told him grudgingly.

'And that's your *home*?' He looked mildly shocked even though he had obviously been expecting something like that from the way she had been attacking him.

'My real home...? I suppose that's where my mother lives, in the village where I was brought up, where my friends are. She lives in a nice house, really. By ordinary standards, that is. A square-built, grey stone country house with roses round the front porch, a garden that tends to run a little wild in summer...and in autumn becomes a haze of gold from the fallen beech leaves...' Her eyes misted.

'You are homesick, Chrissy?'

The softness of the question took her unawares. He had the knack of lowering his voice to a caress when it suited him. She shook herself. 'Yes, a little.'

'You would hate to leave that home for long?'

'I shall probably have to. I go where my work takes me.'

'Here? You would be homesick if you were here?'

'As I'm not likely to be here much longer it's hardly a question I'm losing any sleep over,' she clipped.

'And so now what?' He asked the question that was uppermost in her own mind. But there was a long silence which even Juanita hadn't the temerity to break.

Eventually Chrissy spoke. She said, 'You told me we were going to discuss the next few days. But in almost the same breath you told me I had no choice when I left, or, indeed, where I went to. Then, amazingly, you ask "now what?" Would that I knew, Senhor Montada. Would that I knew.'

Ignoring the irony in her tone, he replied, 'Well, the first thing is, I suggest you forget any further idea of living at the forest house. It would not be good for you to be there alone. Surely you see this?'

When she bit her lip, unwilling to admit the truth of what he said, he went on, 'You can work here if you are intent on fulfilling your obligations to your employer——'

'That's crazy and you know it! How *can* I work here?'
She felt his eyes on her and she added hastily, 'It's
beautiful, and I'm sure your hospitality will be im-
peccable, but don't you see I have to finish off Gavin's
study of that particular area—what could I do here?'

'You are very methodical——'

'I'm trained to be.'

He appeared to be deep in thought and she wondered
what clever twist he was going to come up with this
time—though what his purpose was in practically
abducting her and keeping her a prisoner here she
couldn't imagine. Juanita was looking bored, a pout on
her childlike face getting worse by the minute.

'How long do you need to work in that area, do you
think?' he asked at last.

She shrugged. 'Who knows? The intention would be
to work there until the money runs out.'

'And if there is no danger of the money running out?'

Again she shrugged. 'This is purely hypothetical, isn't
it? It could be another six months to gather all the
relevant information. And then a year, longer maybe,
to collate it and make sense of it.'

'In only six weeks you were barely scraping the
surface?'

'True,' she couldn't help agreeing. 'But it was a beginning. I was simply tying up the loose ends for Gavin's
initial survey. Nobody knows at this stage what we might
find. It's——' her eyes had brightened and she leaned
forward '—it's exciting to know that out there we may
find the cures for most of man's diseases. It's a fascinating trail——'

'Tell me.'

She propped her elbows on the table. 'Well, we already know about the curative properties of sassafras,
smilax and cinchona and many others, but in recent years
cures have been found as a result of discovering previ-

ously unknown plants——' She went on to tell him a little more, wondering how much he really knew, and a little surprised when he seemed to be reasonably clued up about her field of research. 'So you see,' she finished, 'it's pretty important to do everything we can, especially as the forest is being destroyed so rapidly these days.'

'I can assure you *my* forest is in no danger of being destroyed.' He smiled. 'I'll have someone show you over the fruit farms if you're interested.' He went on, 'Have you ever been in a rubber plantation?'

When she shook her head he said, 'Remind me to take you with me. I'm due over there shortly. But now, we still haven't solved this problem.'

'Short of flying me back every day I don't see how we can solve it——'

'Very well. Do that.'

'But——'

'You don't mind helicopters?'

'But the expense? And——'

'I think I can probably take care of that. We will find you somewhere to write up your field-notes here then perhaps you need only go out on collecting trips one or two times more?'

She nodded, her mind still reeling. 'That might be possible.' It was true she had a lot of notes to make after the work of the last few days. Only when they were completed need she venture back again. But how long was he intending to keep her here? Before she could broach the question again, he said, 'I am not happy at the thought of you climbing about alone in the forest. You will at least take someone with you next time.'

Rapidly revising her opinion of him yet again, but at the same time still wary until she discovered what was behind this apparent eagerness to help, she said, 'I think I know what I'm doing.'

'So did your colleague and look what happened to him.'

'He felt ill the previous evening. Perhaps it was something to do with that.'

He got to his feet. 'I'd better ring the hospital. They should be there by now. Excuse me.'

'Come!' It was Juanita. 'I show you your suite. Is very pretty.' Taking Chrissy by the hand, she led her in the opposite direction to the one Rodrigo was taking. She noticed he went through some doors on the other side of the pool and when he folded them back she could see a desk with a woman sitting at a typewriter inside. What a gorgeous place to work, she thought. Then she realised she was going to be in the same boat for the next few days. 'How extraordinary all this is!' she exclaimed to Juanita. She had to remind herself that she wasn't dreaming.

As Juanita had told her, the suite allocated to her was ravishingly pretty and, despite the inevitable humidity, the air-conditioning kept it cool and fresh. Looking round, Chrissy realised it would be far more pleasant to work here than in the lab. She could easily organise it, for, in addition to a bedroom and bathroom, there was a small sitting-room with a useful table and straight-backed chair and there was even a balcony with a view of the pool.

Leaning on the balustrade, she gazed across to the row of palms she had seen from the helicopter, then to the paddock with the horses and beyond that to the limitless dark green of the jungle...

'Juanita?' She turned but the girl had gone out without a sound. She wondered what the pattern for the rest of the day would be—she hadn't even had time to pick up her notebooks, as the helicopter had touched down and lifted off inside a few minutes.

The house was silent and she wondered if it was the traditional siesta-time that had brought this lull in any activity, or whether it always had this brooding silence hanging over it.

Wanting nothing more than to explore her surroundings, she knew it would be killing in this heat. A splash from the pool made her swivel in time to see a dark head break the crystal surface.

It was Rodrigo. With powerful strokes he covered the length of the pool then turned to swim back. As his head came out of the water he glanced up towards her balcony, then he was ploughing powerfully back towards the house. When he got there he looked up again. 'Chrissy, come on down. You swim, don't you?'

She leaned on the balustrade and looked down at him. His striking looks still caused her heart to bump. 'I'm going to lie down—besides I haven't got a swim-suit.' And it's safer up here, she said to herself. But he hauled himself out of the pool and came to stand beneath her balcony. She tried not to stare. He was one gorgeous man, with firm, well-developed muscles, and perfectly proportioned, with the final touch of a golden all-over tan.

'I'll get someone to find you a suit to wear. Don't go away.' To her relief he disappeared indoors.

A few moments later a maid stood on the threshold with a selection of swim-suits. 'Please to try?' she said, pushing them into Chrissy's hands.

Unused to being organised in this way, she nearly pushed the suits back, but realising it would look rude she thanked the girl and went back into her room. He was simply too well organised for comfort, but at least she might as well slip into the suits to see what sort of shape she was in. They turned out to be far more glamorous than the sort of suit she would have chosen—or, more truthfully, been able to afford. They were high-sided and cut to flatter, and she had difficulty in making up her mind. Then she picked the black one with just a slash of green across the top of its boned bodice. Even as the most demure of the three it made her feel like a siren with its laced sides and clingy styling.

Wondering if she could still find an excuse not to go down, she had a peep over the balcony, but Rodrigo spotted her at once. 'Any good?' he called.

'Not bad,' she replied.

'Come on, then.'

Wondering if Juanita would be joining them, she made her way self-consciously downstairs with a white towelling robe slung over her shoulders, suddenly shy at the thought of exposing herself to Rodrigo's critical examination.

He was standing on the edge of the pool when she emerged and strode over to her with an interested smile. 'Well? Did you find one to fit?'

Slowly, feeling awkward, she slipped out of the robe. As it slid to the ground he raised his eyebrows. There was a pause while he seemed to discard several responses that apparently sprang to mind, and finally he simply said nothing, only his expression, a mixture of open approval and something like mischief, showing that he wasn't completely impervious to the effect she created.

He waited until she was standing on the edge before coming up behind her and slipping a hand round her waist pulling her in with him. They hit the water together. It was delicious, like cool satin on her skin, and she struck out for the other end straight away. She could see Rodrigo out of the corner of her eyes swimming lazily along beside her.

They swam about for a good half-hour, having little races then swimming off by themselves before coming back again to race and chase each other again. She was surprised how approachable he could be when he wanted to be—gone was that rather forbidding air of authority he sometimes wore, the pride, the arrogance—he was almost boyish, charming and light-hearted. She wondered what it was for and how long it would last, remembering how changeable he could be.

'Where's Juanita?' she asked as they tacitly turned back towards the house.

'Can you imagine a kitten like her getting her swimsuit wet?' He chuckled. 'She's a little animal, she sleeps, she eats and she plays...'

Chrissy felt an invisible hand squeeze her heart. The word play sounded too innocent for the sort of things she imagined those two would get up to. For a while she had forgotten the existence of any love interest in Rodrigo's life. He was like that, she was beginning to discover. He could make her feel she were the only woman in the world. It was the way he looked at her— the intensity in those cobalt eyes as if she was more than just an unimportant fragment in his obviously busy and complicated life.

She climbed out of the water in a shimmer of sparkling droplets then turned as he climbed out beside her, unable to conceal an involuntary shudder as he put a hand on her shoulder. 'Drink?' he murmured in a voice that was pitched intimately low for such an innocent invitation.

'That would be nice,' she said coolly, moving away.

'It's too hot out here,' he informed her, picking up a dazzling white towel and draping it round his shoulders, 'Let's go somewhere cool.'

Confident there would be servants about, she followed him in bare feet across the cool marble of interconnecting rooms until they came out on the north side of the house where there was a shady trellis-covered patio. It was so pretty with its trailing flowery vines, orchids and a host of other rioting plants that she couldn't help exclaiming with approval.

'I'm surprised you don't see them as just another number on a grid,' he remarked. 'Doesn't being a botanist take away the joy?' He reached out and pulled a pure white orchid from its stem and held it near his nostrils.

'It doesn't spoil it, but I do know that if it's scent you want you should have picked that purple one over there.'

He laughed. 'I chose this because it reminds me of you...' He held it out to her.

She knew she could reject it with a little joke, but she took it from him instead and held it to her face, knowing she would treasure it long after this moment was forgotten. Its creamy heart seemed to hold the light like a pearl. She looked down into its depths wishing she could hold the moment—forever. It was an unexpected tableau.

Confused by the chaos of emotions it released, she stumbled a little as she made for one of the wicker chairs. Fervently hoping he would have the tact to choose one of those placed at a safer distance, she felt nervous when he sat down beside her, stretching out his long legs and even making her turn a little to avoid the danger of accidental contact. Juanita's existence was firmly at the forefront of her mind.

'Are you not used to being given flowers?' he probed. One of the maids appeared as if by magic with a jug of iced fruit juice topped with leaves of dark mint.

'It usually means something when an Englishman gives flowers. It's not an everyday thing.'

'How unromantic.'

She laughed jerkily. 'Yes, I suppose so. But sincere?'

'So you took that to be an act of insincerity just now?'

'No! I mean—well, yes, in one way...' She glanced at his gold ring as he reached over to hand her a glass.

'I meant it most sincerely.' His blue eyes were like the turquoise pool, catching and refracting light, shot through with silver and shadow.

'What did it mean?' she mocked lightly, safe in the protection that gold band represented.

'It meant I admire the beauty of the flower just as I admire the beauty of the woman—you, I mean.' His glance had fallen to her lips and she felt them trembling under his gaze.

'Very pretty words, thank you,' she managed to say. 'The flower is beautiful.'

'But you are probably thinking, this is the man who the other day told me beauty is only skin deep, so the compliment is worth nothing.' He laughed. 'Am I right?'

'I wasn't thinking that, no,' she countered, tearing her glance away. Her lips were burning as if he had done more than merely look at them with hunger in his eyes.

'Of course, there is more to you than physical beauty. I'm learning that. You are quite intrepid. Honest. Proud. A mixture of common sense and innocence.'

'This is like an inventory,' she remarked, embarrassed at hearing herself analysed in this way.

'An inventory of what, I wonder? A good friend, a companion—or something more?' He raised one eyebrow as if expecting her to supply the answer, but he had lost her.

'I'm afraid I don't know where this line is leading——'

'I shall tell you if you really don't know——' again he paused '—and you say you don't?'

Chrissy held her breath for what was coming next.

He said, 'I want to be your lover—I would ask you to be my mistress if it weren't such a quaint word summoning up pictures of schoolteachers or house-maids or scandal.'

She realised he was serious. And that he had gone on talking, making it into a sort of casual remark because he was actually nervous. But he was serious about what he wanted of her. There could be no doubt of that.

Damn his nervousness, she thought as a shoot of anger like a red-hot flame flared along her spine. For the second time provoked beyond reason by something he had said, she raised her hand to strike him. This time, though, she managed to stop herself. Instead she rose to her feet. There was nothing to say that didn't sound melodramatic. But then, they were in a melodramatic situation. It was after all a land given to drama—everything was bigger and grander and more highly coloured than in monochrome old England. The people were more vivid, the plants, the animals, the insects, the flowers—and the passions. She herself had never felt so vibrantly alive.

'*Senhor*, you insult me!' she managed to hiss before she realised she was wrongly dressed for a big operatic scene. With a more natural exclamation of rage she turned and briskly left his presence.

CHAPTER SEVEN

CHRISSY was trembling by the time she realised she was lost in the network of rooms she had stumbled into, but Rodrigo reached her before she could find a way out. The walls were full of paintings in gold frames in a dark Spanish style, horsemen and soldiers and men in black robes whom she took to be his ancestors, and there was an impression of polished leather, dark oak, ormolu and high empty mirrors with diaphanous curtains blowing in the late afternoon breeze.

His expression sombre, he approached down the echoing gallery with his hands out as if expecting her to try to run past him.

'How insult you?' His eyes spoke shock as he reached her side. 'It was intended as a compliment. The most I can do.' His voice was shaking. 'Hasn't it been clear that I will do for you whatever you wish?'

'How can you say that,' she burst out, 'when you've tried to thwart me at every turn and now, just when I was beginning to think you were being——' she couldn't think of a word adequately combining every confusing thing she felt so she said '—when I thought you were all right you say a thing like that and show that everything was designed just to seduce me——?'

'*Just* to?' His expression of shock deepened. 'Is it not important? To be seduced, made love to, honoured by a man who is passionate about you?'

'Passionate? The only passion has been dislike and anger. You even told me you didn't like me!'

'Like? What is that? Like, dislike? We are different. We love. We hate. Yes? You're not lukewarm in your emotions, Chrissy, I've seen that now. That is what I adore about you——'

'But you shouldn't be saying this sort of thing to me——' she cut in.

'Why ever not? It is the truth. Don't you believe me?' The strength of his emotions made his accent more pronounced, as if his voice was the first thing over which he lost control. It made him sound even more attractive, if that were possible, and Chrissy wanted to lean weakly in his arms. With a superhuman effort she checked the urge and stood ramrod straight in front of him, waiting for an opportunity to escape.

'In this country,' he was saying, blocking her exit, 'it is different maybe from yours?'

She couldn't help giving a faint smile.

He grimaced. 'OK, I think you too are sometimes very strange, difficult. Infuriating even. And you think the same of me. But I don't dislike you. Nor did I dislike you when I used that word. I was afraid, Chrissy, don't you understand? I was afraid of where my desire for you was leading me.' He paused. 'I am García Montada— and I was afraid!' He gave an amazed laugh, inviting her to share his astonishment, but all she could feel was guilt—guilt that she should arouse feelings of desire in the heart of a married man, feelings that he—a man with the sense of honour of García Montada—could not control.

He was gazing at her now as if willing her to share his emotions and his voice dropped to a husky, more intimate note. 'I think,' he stated baldly, 'I am obsessed by you.'

He moved closer. Chrissy felt she was going to fall. She swayed slightly but gripped on to her self-control with both hands. Why was he saying this to her? Did he really believe she would become his mistress? It was cruel—it was the most cruel invitation she could ever imagine being offered—her own feelings were in turmoil and she had to snatch her glance away before his will invaded her feeble defences.

He said, 'I put my helicopter at your complete disposal. I wouldn't do that for anyone else. I did it because I want to give you the world. I thought that would be satisfaction enough!'

He ran a hand through his thick mane as if impatient with himself for being unable to explain so she could understand. 'Don't you know,' he went on, 'if that fellow hadn't fallen from a tree giving me the perfect opportunity to bring you back here I would probably have had to push him?' His mouth curved for a moment then his tone roughened.

'I left, telling you I would not return. That was my firm intention. It seemed best to end it there before it got out of control. But I spent an entire night sitting with a drink in my hand beside the pool, thinking, thinking...thinking only of you. I guess I must have willed that fellow out of the tree!'

She smiled. She couldn't tell whether what he was saying was true or not. Probably not, she judged—he was too tough to wear his heart on his sleeve like this. Yet there was something unexpectedly vulnerable in his expression—something that tugged at her heart-strings, for he seemed astonished by what he was telling her, as if he couldn't believe it was happening to him. As if he had never expected to love a woman like this. At least, if he really did love her.

She frowned. That wasn't a word he had actually used, was it? He said he was obsessed by her. He wanted her. No. *Love* was not a word he had used. She bit her lip. Instead of making things clearer he had confused her even more. She was almost swayed by him. He was so convincing. And she longed to believe he felt the same way she did. Yet there was one thing saving her from giving way. It was clear. He was married, and she didn't intend to let the situation go any further than it already had done.

He put out a hand. 'Now come on,' he coaxed, 'let's at least talk it over.'

'But how can I talk over such an outrageous suggestion?' she protested, rallying all her reserves to resist him. 'Probably before I know it you'll have persuaded me it's a good idea!'

He was already taking hold of both her hands.

'Please don't touch me, Rod—I don't want you to.' She drew back with a nervous little shake of her head.

'Ah, so that is what you call me in your dreams!' His fingertips played over her bare arms.

'I don't call you anything in my dreams!' she bluffed. 'How vain to imagine it!' Her knees were trembling. If only he wouldn't touch her like that. Look at her like that. Say such things to her.

'I wish you would share my dreams at night,' his voice vibrated. 'Often I can't sleep and when I do finally drift away it's like heaven, because there I find you—waiting for me.'

'Not so wonderful for your wife——' she managed to blurt.

'Wife?' He gave a shrug. 'A wife is something else. Now please,' he went on, composure fully restored, 'at least come back and finish your drink. You are here for some days, if not weeks, so you may as well learn to talk to me without jumping up every time I say something that surprises you. And you must agree it would have been wrong to hide how I feel about you?'

She couldn't answer.

He was sounding reasonable and in control again and had even removed his hands from around hers.

'I must go and get changed,' she said nervously. 'I would like to have my shirt and trousers laundered...'

'No problem. Give them to the maid. Juanita has found things for you to wear? We are quite informal, but perhaps that swim-suit is a little too sizzling if you wish to keep me at arm's length?' He turned her towards the door she had missed. 'This way. Let me show you.'

He's being a knight again, she registered, as he guided her back through the shadowy rooms to the foot of the marble stairs. Extracting a promise to come down soon so he could show her around the gardens, he left her and, safe in her room, she pulled on a plain black cotton dress with a high round collar and an unfortunate plunging back which she tried to hide beneath a silk shawl. The other garments were even more provocative and she wondered what sort of lifestyle led him to have a supply of new and expensive designer clothes on supply for his female guests.

She also wondered why Juanita was leaving him to entertain her by himself, but she realised she could delay no longer, so, determined to keep him at arm's length, she went down to find him.

He had already changed into a black shirt and a pair of plain black trousers and when he saw she was in black too he began to laugh. 'Perhaps we are not so far apart as we think, *caro*?' He cupped her chin in one hand before she could step back. Then she found it too pleasurable to prevent, and when he kissed her lightly on the end of her nose she realised that her good intentions were not enough.

'Rod, you *know* you shouldn't touch me like this——' she blurted as they walked out through the double doors at the front of the house.

'Would you like me to keep my distance *so*?' He moved about two yards away. 'Safe?'

She nodded. 'Just about.'

'At least you're not telling me I don't have any effect on you. That is a beginning, no?'

'And an ending too,' she told him across the intervening space. 'It can't go any further than this. It really can't.'

'There is someone else?' He came closer. 'This Gavin you've taken over from. Is it he? He is something special to you?' His eyebrows had gone up in astonishment.

Chrissy bit her lip. It might help if he thought her heart belonged to someone else, but she couldn't tell a deliberate lie. Her silence was enough, though, to make him jump to the wrong conclusion.

His light-hearted mood changed. 'You should have told me sooner. I'm a jealous man and I won't *let* you waste your life with a man like that——'

'But you hardly know him,' she was forced to protest. 'How can you say a thing like that about a man you don't know?'

'What is he? A botanist. Does he earn, what, how much?'

'That's nothing to do with it.'

'Aren't you trying to say you're thinking of marrying him?'

She shook her head. 'I've told you what I feel about marriage. I want to be established in my career first.'

'Ah yes, and then you throw yourself away on this nobody?'

'No, not necessarily—look, I'm not going to marry *him*!'

'Not marriage, so he is just someone you pass the time with?'

'*No!*' Even that wasn't true. She had only met poor Gavin once!

'So what is he? Not your fiancé, not your *compadre*...and that leaves only one thing—*your lover*. Is that it, Chrissy?'

'No, of *course* not! You've got this all wrong.'

His face was haggard and she had never seen him look so cold. She put out a hand but he dashed it away. 'No, I don't want compassion. Don't you recognise anger? Really, to think you would consider giving yourself to a man like that—a man with—really, Chrissy. This *cannot* be true.' He turned away.

'Rod, honestly, you really don't understand.'

'I don't?' He gave her a sardonic smile. 'It's more difficult than this? What a labyrinthine love-life you must have.' He walked on briskly, calling over his shoulder. 'Come along.'

He took her towards the stable block. There were fifteen or so beautiful polo ponies, in quarters that shone with care, and she put up a hand to stroke what was evidently his favourite, a grey that whickered softly through its nostrils when they turned to go.

'And now the garden as I promised.' He led at a brisk pace so that she had to hurry to keep up. It was a very brief inspection of the terraces at the side of the house, where roses grew in profusion, but she got the feeling that he regretted offering to show her round and only wanted to get it over with as quickly as possible. She knew he was angry at what he now believed, but it was hardly her fault he had jumped to conclusions, and anyway, he shouldn't even *think* of her like this. It was all wrong.

His aloof manner lasted all through dinner. Luckily a couple of the farm managers had been invited and while Rod addressed a few remarks to them Juanita's constant chatter covered any awkwardness.

Next day Chrissy was flown out in the helicopter to pick up her things from the lab and when she came back one of the maids came to tell her that a room in the office apartment beside the pool had been arranged as a study for her. It couldn't have been more idyllic.

She set her things out on the wide desk beside the open windows and raised the blinds so she could look out. Sun slanted through the row of royal palms at the far end, casting rippling shadows over the empty water. Over on the other side someone was already bringing out a drinks trolley and flares were being prepared for when it got dark. The small fountain, invisible in an inner courtyard, was audible now in the quiet of evening. She gave a sigh of pleasure.

The only dark cloud was Rod. Today she had seen him once when he came out to the helicopter with her—no doubt checking that she wasn't going to hijack it and fly back to the city! she thought. But he had hardly spoken to her. Indeed, he had hardly even looked at her. It seemed if she wasn't going to play his game he didn't want to have anything to do with her. He was behaving like a small boy deprived of a toy. He had probably always had things his own way. It was a major flaw in his character and she told herself that if she kept on remembering it she would soon get over her hopeless physical longing for him, for mere attraction soon palled without anything deeper to strengthen it and make it grow.

The days unfolded predictably. She worked every morning and evening in her study and spent many an agreeable and leisurely lunchtime with the girls who worked in the office next door. Juanita was around for a day or two then came to say goodbye before disappearing in the helicopter.

'Gone to her house on the coast,' one of the girls told Chrissy. She wasn't mentioned after that.

Rod seemed to have retreated into a tower of silence. She saw him, dressed in white jodphurs and a black T-shirt, wearing shiny black leather boots and a hard hat, exercising the horses in the paddock; or, in a drill shirt and army-style gear, leaving the hacienda in a Jeep to visit the plantations; or deep in conversation with his managers in the casual clothes he had worn on their first night here. His bronzed good looks haunted her but he was always moving away in the distance, always busy, always with his attention elsewhere.

He hadn't repeated his invitation to take her out to the plantation with him. She had gleaned the fact that the hacienda started as a rubber plantation several hundred years ago, but that now it was a major supplier of fruit and coffee. She gathered that there were other interests—schools, a hospital—the one where she could visit the luckless Lars as it turned out—and a bank—a network of interests that had grown up alongside the expansion of the fruit business just as a small village had grown up alongside the hacienda in order to supply its needs. There was a butcher, a baker, a cheerful little book store and even a hairdresser, as Chrissy discovered one day when she happened to mention that her hair needed a trim.

One of the girls took her down later that afternoon. It was the first time she had walked further than the grounds of the house since arriving here. Everyone they met on the road gave them a cheerful greeting and when they came to the infants' school a crowd of dark-haired tots ran across the playground to meet them. Chrissy's companion, Anna, lifted one of the children high in the air then hugged him to her. 'This is my own precious one.' She smiled when she deposited him back in the midst of his friends. 'I thank the García Montadas every day of my life for what they have done for me and my family. Things are not so wonderful elsewhere in the world.'

'It's a model village,' agreed Chrissy. 'There's everything you could need.' They chatted to the baker, tasted cheeses at another shop, admired the flower display in the little church and finally reached the hairdresser's.

'You're completely self-sufficient,' she went on. 'No need to bother with the outside world at all.'

'It would be narrow, no, living like that? I like to visit the city maybe twice a year to go to the cafés and the cinema and the dance-halls. See new faces! *El Senhor* spends much time in the city. Maybe you go with him?' She gave Chrissy a quizzical glance.

'I'm here to work, not go gadding about sightseeing!' laughed Chrissy. In her heart she knew she wouldn't even get the chance—flying around in the helicopter with Rod might have been heaven in other circumstances, but as things stood it was the last thing that would happen, and the last thing she wanted!

When they returned to the house her hair had been not only expertly trimmed but piled up in a sophisticated arrangement that was a mass of artlessly falling tendrils—she only wished she had somewhere special to go to show it off! But there was work to be done again after dinner. She thanked Anna and made her way up to her rooms.

A dark shape was just coming out of one of the shadowy inner salons, but she knew who it was from his bearing before she saw him fully. That he hadn't known she was going to be there was evident from the way he jerked to a halt then carried on walking as if too busy to stop. Chrissy's heart turned over. Despite her still smouldering anger with him she couldn't bear for things to have descended to this level of animosity again.

She called out to him.

He had reached the outer door by now and turned with his hand on it. 'I'm in rather a hurry, Chrissy, will it wait?'

'Are you really too busy to——' She broke off, not wanting to reopen things but pushed to say something, if only to express her gratitude for his undoubted generosity.

He changed his mind about leaving and sauntered slowly towards her. 'What's this?' he asked huskily. 'Are you celebrating?'

His blue eyes seemed to glitter as they moved over her new hairdo, taking in every bit of it with a reluctant approval. She put up a hand to touch it, self-consciously pulling at a stray tendril and biting her lower lip. Her breathing seemed to come to a full stop whenever he came near—it was still the same, despite everything.

He took a step closer but she was rooted to the spot. Why had she called out to him like that? How could she have imagined she would feel nothing this time? She deliberately steadied her breathing, but she could feel her nipples tighten in primitive excitement against the thin voile of the dress she wore. Her body was melting at his nearness and she could almost feel his touch honeying over her naked skin.

'Angel—why are you doing this to me? I think you'd better leave——' His voice rasped in her ears and when she stole a look at him his face was a pale mask from which his eyes glittered menacingly.

'Leave?' she gasped.

He shook his head. 'No, not that, I'm sorry. I gave my word. We have our agreement. But something must be worked out to get us through the next twenty-nine days...and nights.' He lifted a black eyebrow, cynical again, and in control, the throbbing intensity of the last few moments replaced by a familiar hardness. 'I'm not used to having a woman about the place who does this to me...' He touched himself on the chest over his heart and gave another thin smile.

As she managed to tear her glance from his he asked silkily, 'This *lover* of yours—why does he not write to you or even phone you? Haven't you told him you can be contacted? Maybe you would like to fax him?'

She turned back. 'You know he isn't my lover, Rod. I told you that.'

'Such a long silence—either you're speaking the truth or he's a fool.'

He regarded her without speaking, and in a flurry of confusion she beat a retreat, reaching the sanctuary of her room with a rapidly beating heart and sitting for a long time looking down at the garden before she knew it was time to go down to dinner and come face to face with him again.

Dinner on the terrace. Guests. Music. The romantic glow of fire-flares softening the contours of faces, bringing a sheen to the hair. A scene from paradise...but anguish in her soul whenever she glanced at him.

He was in black again. It emphasised his predatory sex appeal. Despite his deep tan, the strength in his face, he seemed drained, unfocused, dark smudges beneath his eyes, the accentuated hollows under the cheekbones hinting at fatigue. His restless eyes were over-bright, observing with sardonic detachment the scene in front of him.

He was moving politely from one group to another but there was something in him that remained aloof. Their eyes never met. She couldn't even tell if he knew she was there.

She saw his lips draw back in a brief smile at something someone was telling him. She wanted to run to his side, to reach out and touch the smooth gloss of his black hair. She ached for him despite the coiled and dangerous air he wore tonight. He seemed to vibrate with silent power, a giant in the crowd.

Never has he seemed more remote, she registered. And never more forbidden. García Montada. *El Senhor.*

He has the power of a medieval monarch, she told herself, trying not to allow her glance to be continually drawn his way, but she knew now he ruled wisely and well. Her heart ached with longing for what she couldn't have.

Feeling lost in the surrounding babble, she was helping herself to some strawberries from the buffet when her body gave a thrill of recognition.

He was beside her.

There was no need to turn her head. The little hairs on the back of her neck were suddenly alive with the knowledge.

Her fingers trembled as she lifted a strawberry and bit into it. She swallowed. Waiting.

A tremor ran through her entire body as one firm hand came to rest in the small of her back. The other one held a strawberry to her lips.

'Come, angel,' he murmured huskily. 'We have played too long. Try this. This is the best. Taste and enjoy.'

With still averted glance she had no choice but to surrender her mouth to the succulence of soft flesh. Sweetness oozed over her tongue and trickled deliciously down her throat.

'Good?' he murmured. His thumb was moving at the base of her spine, making tiny movements that were nothing in themselves but turned her limbs to liquid sweetness.

'We are avoiding each other, angel. We are both trying to draw back. How sensible!' His tone was disparaging. 'But what good is it doing? Why live in hell when the gates of paradise are there to be opened?' His voice was now an urgent whisper against her ear.

She half turned.

'There is no one else for you,' he said swiftly. 'This we both know. We know it. And I would make things so beautiful for you...you would be like a princess by my side... Say yes, angel, say yes and put me out of my misery...'

When she didn't answer he went on in the same urgent whisper, 'Come . . . let me choose another strawberry for you. This one—this one is perfect . . .'

Unable to resist, she opened her mouth and felt the rough texture between her lips. When her teeth bit into its flesh it was even sweeter and sharper than the last . . .

'Life can be like this. I can choose the best for you in everything if you will only allow it.'

With a gulp she swallowed the strawberry and felt his hard body pressing against her own as he leaned over to pluck another fruit from the dish.

Forbidden fruit . . .

Her head sank back as she swayed to look into his eyes. The blue of heaven was flecked with the silver of night. 'Don't . . .' She struggled to find her voice. 'Don't taunt me, Senhor Montada . . .'

His thumb was still making its velvety motions at the base of her spine but it was as if he were touching her all over. She regretted the backless dress but had found nothing more discreet. His warm hand on her skin was like a promise of things to come if only she could surrender . . .

She turned suddenly, dashing his hand away. 'Please!' she hissed fiercely, but keeping her voice low so that none of the other guests would hear. 'You must stop this——'

'But why? Tell me your reasons?' he countered hoarsely. 'There is no one else. After days of hell I have discovered that much!'

'Oh, have you?' she whispered. 'Are you sure?'

'I'm as sure as anyone can be unless you have a secret lover no one in the world knows about!'

How true his words, she thought in a fever of confusion. But she mustn't weaken while he wore someone else's ring. 'And how do you know this? What do you really know about me?'

'Naturally I have been in contact with your boss, this Cavendish fellow——'

'You've been spying on me?'

'Not at all. It would have been unreasonable to fly you here and tell no one. Your Gavin is a man twice your age whom you have met once only. Am I right?'

She didn't reply to that but lifted her chin and said, 'So?'

'So I have no need to fear your heart is his, nor your lips, nor——' his voice dropped an interval '—nor anything else I would wish to possess——'

'You're stepping beyond the bounds again and if you don't want me to cause a scene——' she began in a furious whisper.

'Let's not risk that!' His lips curled with amusement. 'I would hate to see you humiliate yourself in front of my guests.' Instead of stalking off as she hoped, he gripped her by the wrists and, clearing a way through the crowd with a convincing smile on his face, hauled her unobtrusively around a corner into the small courtyard off the main terrace. Here a fountain tinkled charmingly out of the mouth of a dolphin into a marble basin full of fish.

He trapped her against one of the walls with a hand each side of her head. It reminded her of the time he had caught her climbing down from the ascent tree and in order to prevent her kicking out at him had pinned her against it. They had almost reached some understanding after that, but now it seemed as if they were back to square one. How could he expect it to be any different when he was married and insisted on trying to persuade her to do something she knew she would always regret?

She closed her eyes to shut out the sight of the lips she longed to submit to. 'Don't do that if you don't want me to kiss you to distraction,' he suggested, his tone hard now. She guessed it was only pride that was keeping him from carrying out his threat.

But she opened her eyes at once. There was a considering look in his own as if he was still trying to understand the mystery of her rejection. 'How can you prefer your empty bed to the nights of pleasure we could share?' he murmured throatily. 'Is it maybe because you have never had a lover before now, Chrissy?'

In the half-light she wondered if he could see the flame that swept her cheeks. But she mustn't let him think she was an *ingénue* or he would regard her as easy game. 'I don't know why you should imagine *that*, Senhor,' she said stiffly.

'Senhor...? That tells me as much as does your intentionally misleading reply.' He lifted one hand and stroked the top of her head. 'I should have realised. I've made every wrong move—when all I wanted was to offer you everything.'

'At a price,' she pointed out in case she found herself swayed by his apparent generosity.

'A price? But yes, and who would pay? Surely not you? How so? In pleasure received, in happiness. I could make you happy, Chrissy. I could teach you how to love. You would pay no price, believe me.'

'And if I didn't do exactly as you wanted you would retreat into your tower of silence again,' she said toughly.

'That, yes. I have tried to ignore you. I thought it was what you wanted. But it is hard, so hard. I have never put myself on the line like this before. I have had no need to. Me? García Montada—yes, I've had things my way. Always. I admit that. And now you, a little angelic creature, say no and my world is in ashes.'

He leaned down and kissed her lightly, then suddenly she felt his hands come up as if he couldn't stop them and she was being pulled heavily against him, her own struggles, violent though they were, doing more to aid than hinder him as he bent over her in a passionate embrace. When he lifted his head from her lips he ground out, 'Why don't you stop me?'

'I—I can't——' she whispered. 'I have to trust you to stop——'

'How? When I am sick with longing for you?' He held her swaying against him and she felt his fingers running over and over through her hair.

'I'm making a mess of your hairstyle,' he told her in a feverish whisper. 'Forgive me.'

'I can't help forgiving you everything but one thing, Rod. You must know that...' She felt tears of anguish glisten in the corners of her eyes. It wasn't fair to be taunted like this—he was inflaming her whole mind with dreams of what it would be like to give herself to him, but it was forbidden and she would go on resisting whatever subtle torment of touch and taste and tenderness he invented.

'What is that one thing? Tell me and I'll do away with it!'

'You must know,' she said. 'I could never be your mistress as you put it. To me that would be the lowest degradation. Can't you understand? It's only because you're so—so attractive to me that—well, put simply, I'm ashamed to say I still find you so...' She bit her lip on the brink of confessing everything, but the knowledge that once she did so the task of resisting would be all the harder made her hold back the words.

'Are you trying to tell me you find me somewhat to your liking? But I know that, angel. I know how you melt when I touch you. I've seen your eyes yearning for my look. I'm not completely inexperienced in these things. Don't you realise that if I hadn't seen all that I would not have persisted in this way? I am not a monster. I can keep my hunger under control when necessary. But when you yearn towards me, when your body seems to flame at the slightest touch, I know as well as you that you want me, desire me—and only something powerful is keeping you away from what you want.'

'You know what it is.' She closed her eyes. 'I could never be a man's mistress. It would be so wrong.'

'I see.' He pressed his face against the side of her neck as if unwilling to part from her but then he moved away, releasing her, dragging himself with reluctance from her side, saying, 'I can offer you anything in the world except that——'

'What?' she asked, breathing raggedly and longing for him to hold her if only for a moment longer.

'That...? Marriage,' he said heavily. 'That is what you are asking of me, isn't it?'

'*No!* I——' She jerked up her chin. 'I wasn't asking that. How could I...? I mean——'

'No, all right, as you say.' He gave a strange smile as if an element of distrust had crept into his thoughts. 'Let's leave it. If those are your terms, very well. Let me get used to the idea.'

'Even you——' she was going to say 'even you can't trouble-shoot your way out of this,' but it seemed pointless to go on discussing it. She moved heavily away, intending to join the party. She was amazed she had been able to forget that there were a hundred people or more only feet away. The last few minutes had put the world a million miles out of touch.

He let her go without protest as if he knew there was nothing further to keep them. When she turned at the corner to glance back he was propped against the wall, leaning on one arm, staring after her, his black bulk standing out starkly against the white stucco. With his face in shadow she couldn't tell what expression it wore, but his eyes were hooded and she knew he was already brooding on a way of getting round what he would no doubt see as merely some new obstacle to his desire.

CHAPTER EIGHT

SUNRISE came as swiftly as sunset—hidden beneath the horizon, the sun suddenly lifted, above the tops of the trees, a swollen scarlet globe. Second by second its warm shafts reached into the world of night and put the shadows to flight. From where she was sitting in a small tucked-away boudoir at the front of the house where no one ever seemed to go, Chrissy couldn't help counting off the nights. Only twenty-seven remained. Was Rod counting them too? She knew if he had meant any of the things he had said, then it would be so.

Bitterness at the sacred vows that parted them had kindled and now hours later burned itself out. What was the point of howling against fate? It was her own fool-hardiness that had led her to plunge recklessly on instead of retreating to safety with a thousand miles of ocean between them. When Lars had his accident she should have gone back to the city too. Everyone would have understood. Her contract didn't provide for the closing of the unit and she would have been justified in getting out. She should have done that because anyone else would have realised Rod's decision to bring her back to the hacienda had an ulterior purpose.

At the time she had been so confused, so lost in the tangle of her own emotions, she hadn't thought to consider his. And if she had known his reasons for bringing her here, would she still have come with him? The little voice that said yes made her cringe with shame. Who knows? she asked herself defensively. I would have done what was right.

Stiff with tiredness but more aware of a deep inner chill, she rose to her feet and padded back down the long silent corridors to her rooms. Too tired to dress and yet too nervy to sleep, she lay down on the bed for an hour, tossing as she had done far into the still hours of the previous night.

At seven a maid brought her tea on a tray. When she left and Chrissy sat up she saw a single long-stemmed rose on the white lawn cloth. There was no message, but its colour told her everything—for it was as deep a crimson as heart's blood.

Wearing a yellow halter-neck sun-dress, and with her hair tied back in a sliver of black ribbon, she was at her desk before the sun was much higher. There was something sweet about this part of the morning, a cleanliness, a simplicity, that made the feverish fantasies of the night recede.

Her work was progressing beautifully and she was pleased she had that as a bulwark against the worst pangs of desire that threatened her peace of mind. Soon she would put in a report to the lab at home, send an update to Gavin, and suggest one or two ways in which she might further the scope of the survey in the time at her disposal. It was a pity she couldn't stay out here longer, but no doubt Gavin would be itching to get back—if further grants could be extracted from the powers that be.

The rapid tapping of the typewriter next door gave her a reassuring sense of normality. If it wasn't for the feeling that Rod had some plot up his sleeve she would have coped, if not altogether happily, with the way things were. Though if she had bothered to probe more deeply, she might have come to the conclusion that she owed her present tranquillity to the knowledge that he was close at hand. It was as well, however, to keep thoughts like that at bay.

'This is beautiful, is it from Rodrigo's special crop?' Chrissy spun round then gave a little smile.

'Anna! You gave me a shock, I was miles away and didn't hear you come in.' She blushed, aware that she had been daydreaming about Rod at that very moment.

Anna picked up the crimson rose and sniffed it appreciatively. Her eyes were thoughtful when she replaced it. Wondering what she was thinking, Chrissy felt a tide of confusion sweep over her. What did the staff think of the generosity their boss was bestowing on her? Did they imagine there were strings attached? She pursed her lips. Perhaps it was usual for him to install his mistresses at the house—whether his wife was present or not! Perhaps the staff no longer found it shocking or even interesting? Perhaps Rod and his wife even had some understanding about this sort of thing? It had been strange that Juanita had left so abruptly.

She decided to find out the reason if she could. 'I'm surprised Juanita hasn't come back,' she began. 'Is she still on holiday?'

'*Deus*, no, though she probably wishes she were!' exclaimed Anna, smiling fondly. 'What an imp she is! No, she is now safely back at college.'

'College? I thought she would have left in the circumstances.'

'Oh, she is not as bad as she makes out,' replied Anna, misunderstanding her. 'At seventeen it's the thing to play at being rather wild, don't you think?'

'She's only seventeen?' Chrissy gulped. She wanted to ask how long she and Rod had been married, but somehow found the question sticking in her throat. How could he treat such a young wife with such scant regard? Or was it perhaps merely a marriage of convenience? A dynastic marriage between two great landowning families? 'Are her family very wealthy?' she asked.

Anna gave her a strange look. 'She is of García Montada,' she said, surprised. 'Didn't you know?'

Chrissy nodded dumbly. That hadn't been what she meant—she didn't need to be told she was the wife of García Montada, but Anna's words, confirming her earlier guesswork, made any other questions superfluous.

'You looked lovely last night, Chrissy,' Anna was going on. 'I envy you your blonde hair. The men couldn't take their eyes off you!'

Chrissy managed to force a teasing glance then, determined to put Rodrigo García Montada right out of her mind, went on, 'You'd get a lot of looks in England,' she said, 'English men go wild over dark, Latin looks like yours!'

'Everybody likes something a little exotic, I suppose!' Anna laughed. 'I myself would love to meet some of your Englishmen, though my poor husband would be most put out to hear me talk like this!'

Anna's words sent a knife wound through Chrissy's heart—for suddenly she saw things from what would undoubtedly be Rod's point of view. He had said he wanted her. Now she believed it. But it was with the avid desire of the collector he wanted her—the addition of a blonde to the collection. She was a fool to pine for him. She gave a grimacing smile. 'You must visit me when I go back home.'

Anna nodded. 'Yes,' and added, 'If Rodrigo will ever let you go!'

Chrissy gulped. 'I'm not a prisoner here,' she said, clutching on to the side of the desk. But she was, she knew she was, if only a prisoner of love. And then she thought, I'm a prisoner in other ways too, for I can't just get up and walk out. I'm completely dependent on Rod's goodwill in the matter of leaving here.

'He is a jealous and passionate man, as I expect you have discovered,' probed Anna gently. 'You will have to put up quite a fight to get away.'

Chrissy got up. Anna, quite unintentionally she was sure, was probing too near the bone. 'I think I've already made it clear to him that my work comes first,' she said firmly. 'As soon as I finish here I have to go back to continue the research I was engaged on at home.' That was, she thought fiercely, if Cavendish didn't make things difficult. But surely by the time she went back things would have blown over and his interest would be engaged by someone more amenable to his jaded charm?

'Men,' she said abruptly. 'I thought I would be untroubled out here——'

'In Latin America!' Anna threw her head back. 'Very innocent of you, I must say!' She leaned against the side of the desk. 'Listen, I came to ask you if you would like to come out to the coast with us this weekend? A group of us will go, taking the children. It will give you a break from all this work. Maybe we get to dance, have a beach party. What do you say?'

Anna had scarcely been gone more than twenty minutes when Chrissy happened to lift her head from her notes to see Rodrigo himself striding round the edge of the pool. He had evidently just come back from exercising the horses and was wearing a tight-fitting black polo shirt and equally figure-moulding white jodhpurs. She had seen him at a distance in this gear but now, as he strode towards her in his perfectly cut black boots, she felt her breath stop.

He came to a halt outside her window and leaned in. 'Are you busy? Can you afford to take this evening off?' he asked without offering any greeting. Considering that the last time they had spoken had been in the courtyard last night when he had momentarily lost control and held her in a heated embrace, he was looking remarkably cool now.

His cobalt eyes flickered over her flushed face. 'You look ravishing. But you can come like that as we shall be well chaperoned and I give you my word I won't lay even the tip of one finger on you. Well?'

The muscles of his neck glistened and her glance ran helplessly over the contours of his shoulders, so broad and well-developed, suggesting a blatant animal power, exacting superhuman effort to resist. He flexed his muscles as if impatient for an answer.

'Take time off?' she repeated stupidly.

'I have to go into the city. You can come. Potter round at company headquarters while I do some business. Then we'll eat at a good restaurant and fly back after that. One of my managers and his wife will be with us at all times. Well?' he repeated briskly. 'Yes or no?'

'I don't know...' She glanced down at her notes wondering how much she dared trust him—or herself if it came to that.

'You need a break from all that damned stuff,' he told her, impatiently glancing at her work, 'and you haven't seen much of the country. We are quite civilised, you know. It's not all untamed forest. We have other things to recommend us!'

'I'm sure you have.' She smiled faintly. 'I should warn you though that, if I do say yes, it won't mean I'm going to say yes to any other suggestions.'

He put one of his hands on top of the window-frame and hung there, grinning down at her. He was momentarily boyish again, a side of him she had glimpsed when they had sported in the pool the other day but which was usually well hidden. 'I know,' he said, 'I promise to behave like an English gentleman. I shall be so full of ice and correctness you will wish for me to be back to my old self.'

'On those terms,' she smiled, unable to help herself, 'I can't help but say yes.'

Her heart was singing as he turned to go. She knew she was playing with fire, but it sounded innocent enough—a manager and his wife as constant chaperons and a straight promise to behave like a gentlemen. How could she resist that?

As soon as lunch was over she was introduced to Isidor and his wife Elena and the four of them made their way across the paddock towards the glistening black helicopter. A surreptitious glance had shown her that neither of the other two had any luggage with them so they were obviously intending to return that night. So far so good, she thought. It was impossible not to feel a qualm or two. But he had given his word. Something told her any doubts would be ill-founded.

Another enthralling ride over the forest canopy followed, with the two men pointing out different things of interest—the rubber plantation, distant hills on which the coffee beans were grown, the looping, lizard-brown river that grew ever wider as it crossed and recrossed beneath their steady westerly flight-line.

An air-conditioned limousine was waiting for them at the landing-pad on the outskirts of the city and they were soon being conveyed along wide tree-lined boulevards towards the centre. It was exciting to see such busy streets, full of brightly clad people and hooting, bustling downtown traffic, after nearly three weeks of forest living with the very different sound, the raucous backdrop of the untamed wilderness in her ears.

It was an old colonial city of elegant white buildings, cool balconies, and long shuttered windows. Banners from some recent feast day were fluttering across the streets, and there were sophisticated cafés and bars, and fashionable boutiques.

'You like it?' asked Rod, swivelling in his position beside the uniformed chauffeur.

'It's lovely.' There was no need to say more because her eyes were alight already.

'I'm afraid we shall have to spend some time at headquarters, but there are kept the archives and other things. You will learn more about the family firm if you wish.' He was watching her carefully. Was it important to him that she express an interest in his company? He was trying to impress her perhaps? But he already knew there was no point. Surely he was convinced by now that she wouldn't be swayed by anything, and certainly not by further proof of his wealth and power.

When they reached the imposing entrance to one of the several skyscrapers downtown she followed everyone up a flight of steps that glinted with black quartzite, only noticing at the last minute the tiny, scrolled name in gold of 'García Montada SA' on the smoked glass of a side panel. Obviously the company was too well known to require a more blatant advertisement.

Determined not to be overawed, she followed the other three inside. Rod's presence seemed to send a *frisson* through the entire building. He was at once surrounded by aides who dogged his every step. He turned when they reached the lift and ushered her in ahead of everyone else. As she passed him he whispered in her ear, 'Enough chaperons even for you?'

Her startled glance made him laugh. She tried to avoid his eye when he stood deliberately close as if only attempting to make room for everyone else in the lift. His cologne, that familiar aroma of vanilla, drifted around her and she was glad there were so many others present so she could indulge the moment without fear of the consequences.

Before he went along to his meeting he got out with her on one of the lower floors and handed her over to a man in a white coat. 'This is the director of our newly opened laboratories,' he told her. 'I think you'll find you have plenty in common.'

Surprised, she watched him step back inside the lift, then the doors closed on his humorous expression and the man beside her was already ushering her down the corridor to a room at the end.

'Why didn't you tell me you had already started a programme of research into medicinal plants?' she asked him later when they were all sitting down to dinner in a roof-top restaurant. There was a breathtaking view over the city which now, at nearly midnight, was agleam with lights like an overturned jewel-box.

'It is all so very new,' he answered her question. 'The paint is scarcely dry on the walls. It is hardly something I wish to broadcast to the world until we have unpacked the equipment from its boxes!'

'It's got an exciting future.'

'I hope so. But who can tell? No one really knows what is a blind alley and what will lead to a financial return. Pharmaceuticals are a relatively new field for us. It has only been in the last fifty years that we have become involved.'

Fifty years seemed a long time to Chrissy, but she could understand that in the time-scale regarded by García Montada it was fairly short. As well as being shown round the lab she had visited the company archives where the history of the company was kept in numerous documents dating from the sixteenth century.

'More wine?' She was jerked back to the present by the quizzical expression in the silver-cobalt eyes looking at her from across the table. He had placed her opposite him, with Elena on his right and Isidor to his left. It meant that their eyes need never leave each other's. Or that they played cat-and-mouse again...

She declined the offer of more wine and pretended to study the carpet of jewels stretched out below them. An aircraft, its red and green lights like ruby and emerald, seemed to float against the velvety backdrop, then it sank lower until it merged with the scattered diamonds on the ground.

'You like cities?' asked Isidor when he heard her sigh with pleasure.

'I like this city from what I've seen of it,' she admitted. 'But I like the rain forest too. It really is so beautiful.' Her heart was filled with momentary regret that she would be leaving all this in twenty-five days more.

'But you must stay,' said Elena, with a quick glance at Rod. She touched Chrissy impulsively on the wrist, 'We would like you to stay.'

As she raised her glance she caught sight of Rod's eyes watching her and for a moment she wondered if this was all part of a plot to persuade her to surrender. He was wasting his time if he thought he could get her to change her mind about their relationship. She gave him a rueful smile. He must know what he was doing. He was too astute not to know. Her glance fell to the gold ring on his finger. The memory of how he had touched her the previous night, gently but possessively, sensitively yet with full knowledge of what effect he was having caused her lips to tremble. Twenty-five days. It was like a life-line, a litany to ward off evil.

There was dancing later and Isidor took a turn around the floor with his wife. Chrissy expected Rod to take the opportunity to get her on the floor and legitimately into his arms, but he appeared to be far away, leaning back in his chair and letting his glance idle over the dancers as if he had forgotten her existence. She followed his example and they exchanged not a single word while the other two were on the floor. When they returned Isidor looked surprised to see them still sitting at the table and at once offered Chrissy his arm. She was taken aback to see Rod immediately invite Elena up. They were laughing a lot and chatting like old friends, weaving expertly in and out of the dancing couples.

'Time to break up the party, friends,' he announced when they arrived back at their table just as she and Isidor returned.

The chauffeur was out in the street as if primed to the second to be waiting. Then they were back in the suburbs within a few minutes and drawing up at the landing-pad in the eerie light of the sodium flares. Chrissy was sleepy and climbed into the by now familiar back seat of the helicopter. But Rod reached out a hand, jerking it away before his fingers made contact, with a gruff, 'Let Elena and Isidor sit at the back. You come in the front with me.'

'But the pilot——' she began, knowing there was only one passenger seat at the front.

'I'm flying us back.' He climbed into the cockpit and buckled on his seatbelt then began all the departure procedures. Chrissy told herself not to be surprised he had taken over. There was far more to Rodrigo García Montada than she had first guessed when he had imperiously ordered them to break their siesta on that first, seemingly long ago, afternoon. She had even suspected he was a bandit of some sort! Now she knew he was a man of honour too: he had kept scrupulously to his promise not to lay even the tip of one finger on her.

She slept later than usual next morning, finally dragging herself down to her study and continuing automatically with some further drawings that demanded a lot of patience but little else.

She had fallen asleep on the flight, lulled by the rhythmic turning of the engines and by the contentment that being close to Rodrigo seemed to bring. But now her senses were tuned to a fine pitch of expectation as the longing to see him took over. Now she knew she could trust him she felt there was less need for the vigilance that had made her keep him at a distance yesterday and the very thought of catching a glimpse of him revitalised every fibre of her being.

So the minute she saw him appear in the doorway on the other side of the pool she went to her office window and leaned out.

'Good morning, Rod!'

He gave an answering wave. 'I've been looking for you everywhere. Stop work and grab a bush-hat!' He started to walk round the pool towards her. She was smiling when he reached her and longed to stretch out her arm and run her fingers through his thick mane of night-black hair, but knowing it was forbidden she contented herself by letting her glance trail helplessly over it instead.

'Come on, jump to it, Miss Baker. I don't have all day. In fact,' he glanced at his watch, 'I have a meeting back here at eleven-thirty, so we'll have to get a move on.'

'What? Another helicopter ride?' Her eyes widened with pleasure.

'Just the opposite,' he replied mysteriously. He stepped back and gave her a lop-sided grin. 'Well? Are you coming or not?'

'But where to?' she asked with a swoop of pleasure at the thought of spending a few hours with him.

'Don't ask questions. It's a mystery trip!'

'Goody!' With a childlike clap of her hands she spun from the window and ran outside to him. For a split second he looked as if he was about to take her by the hand but, apparently thinking better of it, drew back just as she herself froze at the prospect of his touch.

He swivelled abruptly, saying over his shoulder, 'The Jeep's at the front. Come on!'

Obediently she hurried after him, through the cool marble hall to the drive at the front of the hacienda. Already the sun was blazing out of a cloudless sky.

When he swung up into the driver's seat, he opened the passenger door and she scrambled in beside him. 'Do tell me where we're going?' she asked as the Jeep growled to life.

'I've told you. It's a mystery trip. Don't you like mysteries?'

She smiled. 'Sometimes. But only if they're nice.'

'I can assure you this is the nicest mystery you'll get today.' He looked at the sky. 'Think of the most perfect place this side of heaven.'

She closed her eyes. She couldn't say so, but the most perfect place was right here, by his side.

Within ten minutes they were bumping along a track beside the river and in another few minutes Rodrigo brought the Jeep to a halt. 'Now for stage two. Get out.'

Still puzzled as to their destination, she climbed down and, seeing him head for a wooden landing-stage screened by overhanging trees, followed at his heels.

There was a canoe moored below, a mysterious wicker basket at one end, an awning shading the stern thwart. 'You sit there...unless you'd rather paddle us upstream?'

'I won't fight you over it!' Giggling, she stepped down into the rocking boat, being careful to avoid taking Rod's helping hand. When she was settled he climbed in with his back to her and took up the paddle.

Soon they were gliding upstream, propelled by the powerful thrusts of Rod's movements. Chrissy felt free to let her eyes dwell on the supple, rhythmic motion of his body, his muscles expanding and tightening with each downward thrust. Longing for time to stop right there, she could almost believe it had done so as they glided along in a vast green cavern of over-arching trees. All around came the relentless echo of unfamiliar shrieks, of parrots and monkeys and a multitude of other unnameable creatures. It was another world, strange, and primitive, dangerous and wildly beautiful.

She could understand Rodrigo's love for it.

Her heart soared with joy and she told herself it was the magic of the place and nothing else that made her feel like this.

They travelled for a short distance through the more open primary jungle, but soon came to a part that had been cleared and begun to grow back in a wild tangle of vegetation close to the bank. There was a profusion of blossoms, ruby, garnet and sapphire, nature's jewels in a rich, green setting.

Rodrigo soon brought the craft skilfully into a half-hidden mooring and helped her out. He went back to the canoe and returned with the basket under one arm. 'We used to come out here when I was a boy,' he explained. 'The entire household. It would be quite a party. We kids would swim in the pool I'm going to show you.'

He forged ahead along a narrow track, Chrissy following eagerly behind. Within minutes she could hear a faint thundering and as they went on it got louder until it seemed to enwrap them in its embrace. Then the leaves parted and the sticky heat of the forest gave way to a cool mist. Soon there was a welcome breeze and then Chrissy gave a gasp. Just in front of them was a magnificent waterfall, plunging, a glittering band of silver, into the depths of a wide pool.

Rodrigo looked down at her. 'Is this paradise or not?' he murmured. For a moment his eyes seemed full of subtle meaning but she turned at once, opening her arms as if to enclose the whole scene in one rapturous embrace. Tears stung her eyes. The beauty of the scene was more moving because it was a once-only moment. Rodrigo would return here time and time again through the years ahead—while she would leave it after today, never to return. It made her want to cry with an impending sense of loss.

'I love it!' she shouted above the crashing of the water, knowing that what she really meant was, I love you. She felt privileged that he should want to show her one of his favourite places and moved that it was done with no ulterior purpose.

She turned to him with shining eyes. 'This is heaven on earth.'

His mouth twisted. 'I'm glad you like it.' There was a momentary bitterness in his voice but it made no sense to her.

She stood in the shallows. Already her blouse was soaked, moulding itself to her breasts in a way she couldn't help. She saw Rodrigo's eyes flicker over her body and away again. He went at once to a sheltered corner by a rocky ledge and dumped the basket there, pretending to fiddle around with it, his head averted. Chrissy, with a sudden awareness of the danger in the situation, shook off her shoes, throwing them down on the edge of the pool. She waded further into the water.

Her heart was thumping wildly and she knew why. But he had given his word the day before and what was more he had kept it. It was only her imagination that was conjuring dangers out of a look, a smile.

She pretended to be absorbed in admiring the falls, but magnificent though they were it was still Rodrigo who filled her soul.

When he came to stand on the bank she forced herself to chatter about this and that, anything to bring some normality to the wild racing of her emotions. 'It's crazy,' she rattled on, 'the trees are like giant versions of my indoor plants at home! That rubber plant——' she

pointed across the clearing '—it could easily be the one
I have on my kitchen window-sill. Except that it's about
a hundred times as big!'

She could feel his eyes on her. The spray from the fall
had already drenched her. It made her hair hang damply
around her shoulders. She should have tied it back today.
She put up a hand. He was still watching her. 'It's like
looking through a magnifying glass,' she hurried on, with
a catch in her breath as he continued to stare at her. 'It
makes me feel so small, like a figure in Lilliput.' She
gave a shaky laugh.

It was true. She did feel small, completely unreal...as
if she'd suddenly stepped out of the safe ordinary world
of every day into a story-book world . . . where anything
might happen.

He waded through the shallows towards her. 'You look
like a water nymph . . .' he said through the roar of the
falls. Then he gave a sudden laugh. 'At least, without
these ridiculous shorts you would—I mean...' He turned
abruptly.

She watched him climb up the bank and stride across
the sandy inlet to the basket. When he returned he was
carrying a silver flask. 'It's our tradition to picnic here.
So, even though we can't stay long, I thought we ought
to keep up the tradition. Here.' He waded to where she
stood with the icy water foaming around her thighs,
handing her a beaker into which he proceeded to pour
a stream of rose-pink liquid. It rattled invitingly with
ice cubes.

He raised the flask to his lips and their eyes met tell-
ingly over the rim. Then he tilted it and Chrissy watched
like someone mesmerised as the muscles of his strong
throat worked. Tearing her glance away, she followed
his example. A delicious sweetness filled her mouth.
When she'd drained the beaker she forced herself to turn

away. She wanted to behave naturally, but didn't know what natural meant any more.

'Don't go too far,' he warned, speaking from right behind her as she waded blindly towards the middle of the pool. 'You're getting into deep water.'

She gave a shaky laugh and stopped. 'I know that only too well!'

There was silence behind her and, when she dared a glance over her shoulder, his eyes were again full of something and she was forced to drop her glance. But her eyes returned of their own accord as if unable to deprive themselves of the sight of him.

'Don't look at me,' she whispered, her words almost lost in the battling roar of the falls.

He came closer and bent so she could hear the words he spoke. 'We're both already in deep water,' he paused. 'I didn't intend this...'

She could feel his breath against her temple. Trickles of moisture were running between her breasts. She could even feel spray on her eyelashes.

'Still "no"?' he asked hoarsely.

She nodded. How could he ask? The effort to reject what she most wanted lodged like a stone in her heart.

He must have read something of the effort it caused, for with a groan he reached for her and, as if it were happening to someone else, she felt her body propel her into his feverish embrace even as the warnings screamed in her ears.

'Darling, you are so very beautiful,' he murmured, sketching a fiery pattern of kisses over her face and neck.

'No, Rod, we mustn't touch each other like this...' she countered in fevered tones. 'Please don't——'

'I want you,' he replied as if that sealed the matter. His mouth burned hers as he raked it over and over with a sudden conflagration of kisses that left her breathless. Her nerves were screaming with the desire for more, but with a distant, half-dreaming release of control, she felt his hands slide slowly down to her waist and then gently leave her. 'You're right,' he muttered hoarsely in her ear. 'I gave you my word. Just make it easy for me. Be angry with me. Hate me. Fight me. Tell me you love another man. Tell me you hate me, darling. Make it easy.'

He stepped back a pace, and then a second pace, and then he was standing on the bank again, chained to her only by the ethereal atoms that danced between them. She brushed a hand over her damp cheeks, mind so dazzled by the yearning need shaking through her that she could have sunk down in the gushing waters and allowed herself to be consumed—as if their desire were something commanded by nature. But he was moving away now.

'Let me show you some flowers you won't have in your collection,' he called. His manner had changed. It was determinedly practical. She knew he didn't feel brusque, that it was a defence against the emotion that threatened with the unconscious force of a natural phenomenon. But she welcomed the chance to draw her tattered defences together.

He was right. They were in deep water and neither of them wanted to be swept away by it.

She followed him up the bank to the side of the cliff, then, watching where he placed his hands and feet, she began to scramble after him. At the top was an endless vista of forest trees, stopped only in the far distance by a ridge of snow-capped mountains.

'This is spectacular,' she breathed. 'Oh, Rod, how wonderful to live amid such splendour.'

'You *say* that——' he began harshly, then checked what he had been about to say and turned abruptly, though not before she had seen his face harden. 'Look, this is what I wanted to show you,' he announced before she could make sense of that look. Following his outstretched hand, she saw a cascade of multi-coloured blooms in a hollow between the rocks.

'This is the only place I've ever seen them,' he told her. 'Do you know what they are?'

She reached out and touched the slender bell-shaped flowers. 'They're beautiful, quite unknown... each one different.' Some were double bell-shaped, others crimped and frilled, yet others so fine they were almost transparent.

He allowed her to choose one or two specimens to take back. She asked, 'Do they have a name?'

He smiled, a sadness in his eyes as he watched her hold the blooms to her face. 'We call them Angel's Wings... It makes sense,' he said as he turned. 'They only grow here... at Paradise Falls.'

He held her hand as they made the awkward journey back to the bottom of the cliff, releasing her as soon as he saw she was safely down. 'Now we must go back,' he told her at once, 'before I miss my appointment.' His eyes lasered briefly over her upturned face, but before it could become the first step on another forbidden path, he hoicked the basket on to one shoulder and set off briskly through the wood.

Chrissy gave one last lingering look over her shoulder at Paradise Falls. She would never forget it. Only the knowledge that their love was forbidden had prevented its becoming a paradise indeed.

With the precious memory stored in her heart forever, she climbed into the canoe and allowed him to propel her back to the busy world beyond.

He left her on the steps of the hacienda. There was an air of something like coldness between them now and she knew she had failed him. He couldn't see anything wrong in her responding to the love he offered. It was an obstacle between them that nothing would remove.

It seared her mind to know that he could not understand
how much she cared. But it was best like this. He still
wore the eagle-crested ring.

She heard the Jeep come roaring back through the
archway halfway through an afternoon that had turned
uncomfortably humid. From her vantage-point in the
shady little boudoir on the first floor at the front, she
saw him climb athletically from the driver's seat and
make for the house.

He found her in the boudoir a few minutes later.

There was a doubtful expression on his face as if he
had something to tell her. Obviously he had come to a
decision of some sort.

While he was standing in the doorway it started to
rain in large hand-sized drops, and within a few minutes
the drive below the balcony had changed from pale
yellow to deep ochre.

Since she had seen him climb out of the Jeep he had
changed out of his khaki work clothes and had donned
a simple white vest with baggy designer trousers. She
wondered how anyone could make such simple attire look
so stylish. His hair was wet as if he had taken a quick
shower before coming to her, and it hung glossily past
his ears, even longer now than when Juanita had teasingly run her fingers through it.

'You've found this little place, have you?' he began.
'It used to be my mother's favourite corner.' The rain
was still drumming on the ground outside and she could
hear it beating on the roof with an increasing tropical
tempo.

Her head lifted. He had never mentioned his family
before. 'I can see why she would like it,' she replied.

'So can I,' he replied at once. 'It gives a perfect view
of the road leading away from this place.' His mouth
twisted with long-held bitterness.

'Did she want to—I mean——?' She was confused by the unexpected savagery of his tone.

'She wanted to. Like me she counted. But for her it was years not nights, and it was years to the time she would escape, not, like me, to a departure that fills me with despair.' With a sudden muffled curse he jerked away. 'It's no good!'

'Wait! Rod——! I mean...' Her eyes searched his face for clues when he swivelled to face her.

He came back, his face a mask. 'Do you know why marriage is out of the question for me?' he almost snarled. 'Because of her. It's been drumming in my head all day... ever since we went to the Falls... I wanted to take you there, to draw you into my past. Make you want to be part of it. But why? What's the purpose when I know—we both know—it would never work out?' He strode to the balcony and looked savagely out at the ceaseless rain. 'OK, so I should rethink perhaps?' He spoke half to himself, but then he gave a fierce shake of his head. 'One day, maybe. Who knows?'

He strode back to where she was sitting and stood over her, a variety of emotions playing openly over his strong features. 'But it wouldn't be with you. Impossible with you. You are wrong for me on every count. You can never be of García Montada.' He was on the point of muscling his way out again when she gave a strangled cry.

Before he had entered the room she had been at peace, or as near as could be with the days dwindling so rapidly to nothing, but now, with a few short sentences, he had shattered the fragile edifice she had built up and the pieces lay in fragments, defying her ability to put them back together.

'What do you mean?' she cried out, half rising from the quilted chair in which she was ensconced. 'I know I can never be "of García Montada" but I've known that from the beginning.' Her voice shook, and when he seemed to be on the point of shouldering his way out without properly explaining his strange remarks, she quavered, 'What have I to do with your mother, Rodrigo, and why have you never mentioned her before?'

He came back, towering over her, face tight with an extremity of emotion she had never seen before despite the intensity of previous encounters. 'Her name is never spoken here,' he said simply. 'My father forbade it.'

'Your father died some years ago, didn't he?' she asked, struggling to understand.

'Have you heard how he died?' he demanded harshly. 'The story the people tell about Miguel García? His lingering death from a broken heart?' A bitter laugh was forced from between his lips. By now the rain was drumming in one consistent roar, almost drowning out his voice but failing to conceal the undeniable anguish in it.

Chrissy shook her head. 'I've heard nothing.'

'No, they are waiting for history to repeat itself,' he told her with bitterness in his tone. 'Afraid perhaps that if they speak out they will bring down the same curse on my head.' His lips whitened. 'Or perhaps they wonder why I don't use you to wreak my revenge on someone who can only arouse bitter memories for this house.'

By 'house' she at once understood him to mean the dynasty of García Montada. 'But what happened to make such a thing a possibility?' she gasped. 'How am I involved?'

'You are not. At least not directly. But sometimes the people take fanciful ideas into their heads and at times even I—in the empty night hours—feel that maybe they are right. She brought him luck, my mother, so they say, and great happiness...and then she took it all away when she left.' He turned as if unable to look at her.

From over by the balcony, with the sheets of rain as a backdrop, he went on, 'All he had after she ran away was me—a child of seven. I lived with his heartbreak from that day on. Seven years. Twice seven years he waited, pacing the drive down there,' he gestured with one shoulder to the front of the hacienda, 'waiting, waiting—always waiting—for a woman who forgot him the minute she tasted the freedom of the outside world. At least...' his voice became far away '...she thought it was freedom. But who knows, perhaps later she longed to return to the forest, but pride would not let her come crawling back to beg his forgiveness?' He raised his dark head. 'Or is that romantic rubbish, Chrissy? Tell me. You should know. You look like her. You come from her world. You of all women must know how she thought about us.'

'I?'

'She was the outsider here. The foreign bride. But it was we who were the foreigners finally when she cast us off.'

He sat down suddenly in the chair opposite and put his head in his hands. 'Her actions have always been inexplicable to me. Why should she punish me? Our family has been one cursed by ill-fated marriages. But it was a double-edged curse. With every bride who fled the primitive solitude of the forest, or died from loneliness, the García Montadas flourished from the union. I'm the heir to a bitter harvest. I made a vow long ago not to tempt fate by an ill-considered love liaison. For me it would be a marriage of convenience or nothing. The vagaries of the heart would not be heeded.'

'But Rod—Rodrigo——' she put out a hand '—I thought you were married? I thought——' She felt dizzy with the effort to take in what he was telling her.

'Married?' His head shot up. 'To whom?'

'To Juanita of course!'

'Ha!' His expression lightened for a moment. 'Are
you mad? She is my niece—family. We wear the rings
of García Montada.' He held up his finger. 'She is a
mere child. A flirtatious little girl. What do you take me
for?' He leaned back and mirth briefly overcame his
earlier bitterness, but then his eyes clouded and he leaned
forward to peer into her face. 'Is *this* what you were
trying to tell me—you could not become the mistress of
a married man?' He paused and when she nodded he
went on, 'You seriously think I would offer you that
sort of liaison? Chrissy—Christine...' He rose.
'Seriously...?'

When she nodded again he furrowed his brow. 'So,
that explains your peculiar reluctance to enjoy what little
we might have shared... How ironic.'

He was standing upright now, storm and shadow
bringing into sharp relief the contours of his body. For
a moment they looked at each other, she with her head
tilted to his, he erect, his face inclined slightly to gaze
down long and gently into her widening eyes.

Slowly he began to shake his head. 'What mischance
and mismatching here. Would our fate have been
changed but for a mistake like that?' He gave a dismissive shrug of his shoulders, 'Well, there it is, my
angel. My decision. Now you know why I cannot offer
you marriage——' He gave a bitter smile. 'I can offer
only the doubtful pleasures of unwedded bliss.' He
shrugged as if the conclusion was foregone. But his eyes
softened as they turned full on hers. 'We are beginning
to learn each other a little... It is bitter knowledge, yes?'

There was a crack of thunder as he turned to go.
Chrissy watched him with staring eyes, even now unable
to put the pieces together so that they could be handled
without hurt.

Fate, she murmured to herself after he had left. Did
they have to submit to its blind force? She glanced out

into the deluge and could just make out the road leading away from the hacienda.

It must have been a view that had brought tears to the eyes of Rodrigo's mother many a time, but her own tears now were not from the longing to escape, but from the hopeless desire to remain.

CHAPTER NINE

SO RODRIGO was a free man. Or as free as a man cursed with the dynastic responsibilities of the García Montadas could be. Yet instead of clearing the air, as the storm had cleared the air of the forest next morning, the knowledge had brought with it the potential for further tempests.

With his open rejection of her in marriage—the possibility of that had never entered Chrissy's imagination—there was also the destruction of the safety barrier that had so far kept them apart—that of imagined marriage vows. She knew he would find it difficult to understand her reasons for continuing to say 'no' in what were for her changed circumstances.

It made her tremble to think that all she had to help her curb her deep longing for him were just the simple precepts she had been taught as a child—never to compromise and never to live in such a way as to be unable to hold up her head.

With no defences left how would she withstand his continuing pursuit? She went to the office next morning and sent a fax to Cavendish demanding her immediate recall. She would repay the grant she had been given to come out here, she would look for another job if that was the price she had to pay. But one thing was certain, she could not trust herself to keep Rodrigo at arm's length any longer. She loved him. She wanted him. And the only barrier was her common sense. That, at the moment, she held as lightly as a bubble.

When he failed to put in an appearance at dinner that evening, having been absent throughout the day as well, the tension of pitting herself against an invisible enemy began to show. She retired early to bed with a headache, then tossed and turned all night in a fever of longing, cursing her inability to get up and take herself brazenly along to his room whatever the consequences, and glad, next morning, when common sense had once again ruled the night.

'Are you feeling unwell?' Anna had stopped by her study for a mid-morning chat and now peered anxiously into Chrissy's pale face.

'I got a headache last night and can't seem to get rid of it,' she replied, almost truthfully. Headache, heartache, it was much the same thing.

'I'll get you something. You of all people should know a cure.' Anna disappeared and a moment later returned with a steaming mug. 'A cup of *maté*. That should do the trick.'

Dutifully Chrissy drank the not unpleasant liquid and thanked Anna for her trouble.

'Don't forget the beach trip tomorrow,' Anna reminded her as she went out.

He was absent again the next day. A fax had come for her during the night. It said simply, 'Stay put, discussions pending.' Mystified and dogged by a strange listlessness, she left it to sort itself out. She seemed to be moving under water now. Nothing was real. A part of her seemed to be missing, part of her mind, her soul, her heart, she didn't know. But she was only half alive. Why had he deserted her now when she needed him? At least they could have talked. Surely they could have talked?

That afternoon when the whole house slept and he had still not returned from wherever he had escaped to,

she did the only thing she could and went along to the
library he had shown her along the same corridor as his
mother's boudoir. There would be something here to
satisfy the nagging questions that were sapping her
vitality. Here there must be at least a passing reference
to the events that had grown into the sort of burden
Rodrigo was carrying.

There was a smell of old leather and vellum. In the
city the archives had dealt exclusively with the business
interests of the family but here they were of a personal
nature. Lists of births and deaths, descriptions of
wedding feasts and christenings, funerals and commem-
orations down through the ages echoed the roll-call of
the dead. The name Rodrigo recurred over and over again
as the name of the first-born son. Chrissy could feel the
weight of it on her shoulders and she cried inwardly to
think that now it wasn't just an imagined barrier that
separated them, but the many barriers of history, of
centuries-old tradition, of the precedent of law and duty.

Then she found the book printed on modern paper,
some of its pages still uncut. Here were the records kept
by Miguel García from the date on which he became
head of the family. Here were private handwritten notes,
the pages of a diary, letters, photographs.

She gazed for a long time at the faded portrait of a
woman like herself only in that she was blonde. There
was a heart-rendingly familiar look about the eyes and
if the photograph had been in colour she knew they
would have been that shade of cobalt she had come to
love.

There was a wilfulness around the mouth that too was
not unfamiliar, but, contrary to what Rodrigo had
hinted, she didn't have the air of a cold woman, a
heartless woman who would abandon her husband and
son on a whim.

Perhaps, thought Chrissy, she was driven by love of her own people to return once for a last goodbye. Perhaps she intended to return here to these foreigners, to this foreign land. How could they ever know? Why did the father and the son not know? What sort of farewell had it been? The black border round the last entry in which she was mentioned told her that now no one would ever know the truth.

A sound in the corridor made her close the book and put it back where she had found it, wondering as she did so whether Rodrigo ever came to look at the portrait of his mother and, if so, what emotions coloured his thoughts. She knew they would have to talk and could scarcely wait for his return.

The last thing she desired that weekend was a beach party. Surrounded by crowds and expected to play her part, she put on a brave face, played handball with the tots, swam, fell off a sailboard once or twice, and later danced with several of Anna's handsome smiling brothers, but, underneath, her heart was an aching void.

They returned in a laughing mêlée in a couple of Jeeps and one or two private cars and disgorged at around three a.m. on the steps of the hacienda amid loud shushing noises and stifled giggles. Chrissy was the only one staying in the hacienda and when everyone climbed back into the vehicles she realised she had been privileged to have an escort to the doors. When everyone drove off again in a chorus of goodnights and stylishly screeching tyres, she was smiling half-heartedly as she watched them go, then turned towards the steps.

A shaft of light cut a swathe through the night. And silhouetted at its centre loomed a black figure.

Fear was her first reaction. He was back. But he was so still. So brooding. Cloaked about with such an air of menace. The light behind him dazzled her eyes. She could only see a shape without detail. Treading the steps to the top, counting them in order to hold still the abrupt racketing of her heart, she drew level. He side-stepped to let her pass.

'Had a good time?' he grated above her ear. Then one hand shot out catching her by the nape of the neck and dragging her to a stop.

'I—I thought you were away,' she blurted, confused by the violence of his expression now she could see his face clearly.

'As you see,' he grimaced, 'I have returned. I hope it doesn't spoil your fun?'

'Anna asked me to go with them a few days ago,' she stammered, wondering why she was bothering to give an account of herself.

'Good. I'm glad to see you're paving the way to being part of the work-force.'

'Sorry?'

'Have the details come through yet?'

'What details? And please, Rod, you're hurting me a little bit——' In fact he was hurting her a lot but she wouldn't give him the satisfaction of knowing that. The look on his face was primitive, savage. He looked as if he would like to hurt her in far worse ways, and put next to the pain in her heart caused by his absence she would prefer any mild physical discomfort to that. But it still needed pointing out.

'I'm sorry.' He immediately released her. 'I didn't realise...I thought you were just going to go sweeping straight past without a word.' He put out a hand and rubbed the back of her neck, then bent to touch it with his lips, straightening abruptly and pushing her inside the house. He closed the massive wooden doors and bolted them, making her feel like a recalcitrant teenager though she'd never had to face the ire of a father after a late-night party before. He swung to face her. 'Hasn't your lab come back with their decision yet?'

'I'm sorry?'

He examined her blank expression. 'You don't know a damn thing about it, do you?'

'Should I?' Vaguely she remembered Cavendish's exhortation to stay put. Discussions pending, whatever that meant. 'Has something been going on?'

'Yesterday, when I saw how interested you were in what we were doing at headquarters, it occurred to me you might consider joining the company on a more permanent basis as a research assistant. Actually it's an idea that's been brewing in my mind for some time. You could still maintain ties with your old job. I thought it would be useful to make it a joint venture, pool resources. They obviously have more advanced facilities in some respects than we have at present. But we have the natural resources—and at the moment we have you.' He smiled grimly. 'I expected a response by now. And I thought you might have already mulled it over and come to your own decision.'

'I...' Her mind raced. 'It sounds a good idea in outline. I would have to know more about it——' To be here, with him. That was what he was offering. Her mouth went dry.

'Of course you need the facts. I have a proposal...' He pounded a fist into the palm of his hand. 'Most definitely *not* a proposal—I'm sorry...' For the first time she saw a look of unmistakable guilt flash across his face, but he recovered and went on, 'I have an outline, I mean. It's in my study. Too late to look at it now, but first thing in the morning...' He hesitated. 'Chrissy...understand what I've had to do.'

He gave her a searching look, his eyes almost storm-coloured as if he was expecting trouble. His lips tightened aggressively. 'We'll talk when you've told me your decision. I'll go over to the office and see if there's a fax waiting. I haven't been back long myself.'

Wondering where he had been for so long, she watched him swivel and, without looking at her again, make his way across the entrance hall to the far door. When he reached it he half turned to find her standing where he had left her. 'Go to bed now. Goodnight,' he told her bleakly. Then he was gone.

Slowly finding her way upstairs, Chrissy could see no explanation for that look of guilt she had witnessed, nor any reason for his brusque, in fact dismissive, manner, especially as what he was telling her sounded like another instance of his generosity. To have first offer of a job like this was a wonderful opportunity. It sounded perfect in every way... Except that it would make the task of keeping him at arm's length impossible... but then... maybe she would find a way of loving him... of being with him... and keeping her self-respect too...?

She brushed a hand across her face. It was all too complex.

First she would have see what Cavendish said.

If he agreed to the plan, time then to unravel the knot that was strangling her heart...

She started to ready herself for bed but something was nagging at her. There was something wrong. She felt it in her bones. It wasn't just that the plan sounded too good to be true—careerwise that was. There was something else.

Even as she went over everything again she could find no fault in it even though she knew something wasn't right.

But it was no good making guesses. She would have to control her misgivings till morning.

Sleeping late, she was eventually wakened by the sound of the single bell from the village church. She lay for a

long time listening to its half-sad, half-merry sound,
imagining the passing centuries when this same sound
had rung out from the white bell-tower over the domain
of Rodrigo's ancestors. She had learned that the village
was known simply as the *aldeia* and in full as *aldeia*
García Montada. His name was branded on everything.

Curious to discover more about the scheme he had
briefly mentioned last night, she went down to the
poolside office to see if he was there. All she found was
a sheaf of notes and the reply from Cavendish.

It was long and detailed but the message was summed
up in the final sentence: all systems go! She gave a
frightened smile. So it was now up to her. Her moment
of destiny approached. She could burn her bridges, or
say no and run for her life.

There was another fax addressed to her—Rod had
placed it so she could see it on top of the outline he had
left out. It was from Gavin. He told her that Cavendish
had tried to persuade him to try for the job himself but
he wanted Chrissy to accept as she had obviously got
the magic touch. She smiled. He was a sweet man.

He was, he said, more than content to know he had
security of tenure as a researcher—there were still, he
went on, a lot more trees in the forest! He finished by
thanking her for sending on his completed findings so
quickly and telling her that he would be seeing her soon.

She took the typescript and settled down beside the
pool to read it. With no one around she soon scanned
the salient points and realised that Rod had been very
thorough. There was nothing she could fault. If his
feelings for her had prompted him to think of a way of
keeping her here, at least his mind had been functioning
properly when he had come to make his proposal—she
bit her lip—to write his outline, she corrected. No wonder
Cavendish had jumped at it. Trust him, though, to try

to push Gavin into the hot-seat and drag her back to the UK!

The turquoise water was lapping invitingly at her feet and, taking the file back to the office, she decided that as she obviously had to amuse herself this morning she might as well take a dip. Going up to her room, she pushed aside the black swim-suit in favour of a tiny gold-thread bikini. Feeling that she might as well dress up as it didn't seem to matter if she dressed down—Rod's ardour wasn't in the least diminished by her deliberate lack of allure—she wriggled into it.

It was extremely revealing. She bit her lip. Dared she? But Juanita's bikini had been just as brief so it was obviously considered to be the done thing to go around so scantily clad. It was a private house, after all. And besides, he had seen her in the black swim-suit before and too many times she had appeared at her worst in stained working garb. This other one was flattering to her figure and she knew it would please him.

Trailing a towelling robe and wondering where everyone was this morning, she made her way downstairs and plunged into the pool with a gasp of pleasure. It was heaven, floating on a translucent cloud, sky and water a matchless blue...reminding her, always reminding her of the heavenly blue of his eyes... She was trembling with anticipation. When he came back she would tell him what she had decided. Then her future would rest in the hands of fate.

'Chrissy!' A peremptory shout cut across her daydreams and she lifted her head, disturbing the lazy star-shape she made on the surface of the water. *He was here. At last!* Her heart bucked. She sank back, a languid mermaid with her long hair floating in a fine mesh around her head. Now she would have to go to him...and tell him...

'*Chrissy!* Get the hell out of there!' There was a muttered aside and when she raised her head again she saw that he was not alone. There was a woman with him dressed entirely in black. Black shoes. Black stockings. Prim black dress with the glint of a gold brooch at the neck. And a fine black veil obscuring her face. She carried gloves, a neat bag and a small black book. Rod, now she looked at him properly, was wearing a solemn black suit with a white shirt and black tie. And now she really looked at him, his face was as black as a thundercloud.

She bobbed upright, treading water, still half in and half out of her daydream.

'Get out, will you? Can't you hear me?'

'Why? What's wrong?' She swam smoothly to the edge with her long blonde hair trailing behind her and bobbed up and down, looking from his furious expression to the impassive veiled countenance of his companion. She could just make out the dark shape of the woman's eyes. They were staring as if in shock.

'How dare you? Get out this minute and clothe yourself!'

Wondering if something terrible had happened, she swam to the side and climbed out, shedding splinters of crystal drops, the sunlight glinting on her gold bikini, her hair snaking around her shoulders, a wild, blonde mane. She bent to squeeze the water out of it then lifted it to the top of her head, holding it there for a moment as she smiled expectantly into his beloved face.

'It's heaven in the water, Rod, why don't you come in?' she gasped. Warm trickles were still running down her shoulders and between her breasts, making her squirm with pleasure. On seeing her rise out of the water like that his eyes had begun to skid feverishly over her almost naked body, desire blazing out of their depths without disguise, and his lips parted in an audible gasp like a man momentarily winded. For a moment time seemed to stretch and everything but his naked desire and her unashamed affirmation of it swung out of focus.

'*Deus!*' It was the snapped exclamation of his companion that brought them both to their senses. The woman in black turned with a swish of starched skirts and made for the house.

'Cover yourself decently then come down to the salon at once!' he barked, turning to follow the woman inside.

Chrissy blinked as she gazed after him. What had all that been about? Then she realised they must both have just returned from church. Even so, surely it didn't warrant this raging reaction as if she had been caught doing something cheap? If the bikini was a little revealing she could hardly be blamed for that—it was one he had provided!

Angry at being made to feel she had done something shameful, she pulled on her robe and marched inside. Why the hell should she go and change? She might want to continue her swim, mightn't she? Or was swimming inexplicably forbidden on a Sunday?

She found the salon—or rather, she was led to it by the sound of a woman's angry voice. Unable to understand what she was saying, there was no doubt as to the gist. An insult had been received and Rodrigo was being informed of that fact in no uncertain terms. She didn't wait to find out how he would respond to it, but instead marched straight inside in her bare feet with the white towelling robe tightly belted and her head held high.

'You wanted to speak to me?' she demanded.

Rod swivelled, his face paste-white, eyes black in their sockets, the skin over the aristocratic nose tight with fury. 'I told you to dress yourself——'

'But I haven't finished my swim,' she cut in. 'Surely you don't expect me to go up, shower, dress, come down, chat, then go up and climb back into my bikini again?'

'You will as long as you're a guest in my house!' he snarled. 'I'm not having you parade around naked in front of Maria——!'

'I'm so sorry!' she exclaimed sweetly. 'I've never noticed you object to my naked body before——'

'I haven't had chance to object as I've never yet managed to get near it——' he grated.

'How disappointing for you!' She realised now that Maria, if that was the name of his temporarily silenced companion, didn't understand a word of what they were saying. 'It's obviously not what your friend thinks!'

'Don't goad me, Chrissy. You've upset her. I demand an immediate apology!'

'Demand? Did you say *demand*?' Her mouth opened in shock.

'You heard me. Do as I say, will you?'

'I don't think so!' she exclaimed in hauteur. 'Why on earth should I? Am I some sort of lackey to be ordered to grovel at your feet? I might remind you I'm not on your payroll *yet*!'

'I demand an apology and refuse to continue this futile conversation until I get one!'

'Don't be ridiculous!' she exploded. 'Apologise for being myself? I've nothing to be ashamed of! How *dare* you try to order me about? I might just as well ask you and your friend to apologise to *me* for disturbing my swim! I was having a *wonderful* time until you two came barging in without warning!' Even she thought it was pushing it to criticise him for walking beside his own pool, but the unexpectedness of his condemnation made her see red. One slim, black glove plucked at Rod's sleeve and a stream of words gushed from behind the veil.

'*Momento,* Maria.' His tone was noticeably less peremptory, but when he turned back to Chrissy it hardened again. 'Get upstairs! Do as I say, damn you!'

'I'm surprised you're not offering to accompany me!' she yelled as she stood her ground.

His control snapped and he lunged towards her with the speed of a panther, but the woman's high-pitched cry brought him to an abrupt halt. *'Get out!'* he ordered in a hoarse whisper only inches from her face. 'Just get out. And when you *do* come down you're going to apologise if I have to force you to your knees to do it!'

'You must be mad!' she cried out as she backed towards the door. 'Who the hell do you think you are? You may be a little tin god in this forsaken backwater, but you're a total *nobody* in the outside world!' She shot a savage glance towards the woman who had taken a little black fan out of her bag and was whisking it rapidly back and forth as if the very air surrounding Chrissy had been contaminated in some way. 'I guess it's *her* doing, isn't it? You would never tell me off merely for having a swim if she weren't here! Far from it! So what's it all about? *Who is she?* What's so special about *her*?'

He moved a pace towards her, face stark, eyes like ice-chips. 'As from today,' he intoned, 'she happens to be my fiancée. For that reason her wishes are to be respected.'

'*Your...?*' Chrissy took a step back. 'I don't believe it... You can't...'

He was staring at her as if willing her to go, his lips white, the hollows beneath the jutting edge of his cheekbones dragged deep like those of a sick man.

With she knew not what resource of inner strength, Chrissy managed to draw herself up, and with a slow, smouldering final glance that spoke more profoundly than any words, she pivoted and made from the room.

* * *

Fiancée? The word pounded in her head with the destructive force of a sledge-hammer. It couldn't *be*. But *why*? Why had he done this? Only days ago he had told her why they couldn't marry. But there had been no mention of an impending engagement to anyone else. Why had he not told her? And why, given that he had done this terrible thing, had he arranged for her to become an employee of his company?

With sickening clarity she thought she understood. He had warned her marriage was out of the question. But he still held out the hope that she would become his mistress—despite his denial that he would ever expect that of her! He had lied then. Tried to disarm her. Make her think well of him. So that he could all the more easily manoeuvre her into a position where she would be unable to say no!

The snake! she stormed in the privacy of her room. And how easily she had talked herself to the very edge of saying yes! He said he knew how she felt about him— and that made it all the worse, for he had cynically played on her feelings, while all the time hoping to satisfy his own undeniable lust.

Hate in a maelstrom of grief and betrayal threatened to overwhelm her. She paced back and forth, back and forth across the marble floor, oblivious to the knock on her door, to the sound of people going on to the terrace, to the lunch gong, to the murmur of dining guests, pacing back and forth in a torment of lost dreams and yearnings and a thousand unanswered questions.

At last, taking a hold on herself, she dragged to a halt. It was pointless hoping to make decisions in this frame of mind. Should she go, should she stay? She felt only the desire to scream and cry, to lash out in fury at the man who had so hurt her. But time would heal, she told herself feverishly. Now I simply have to live each moment as it comes. Think only five minutes ahead, only five minutes to the next thing I have to do.

She forced herself to the cupboard and took down at random one of the dresses that hung inside. Yes, that was it. Dress. Brush her hair. Put on an expression of complete indifference. And go down to lunch. And make polite conversation. And smile. And never, *never* let him know how he had all but destroyed her. She would not let him know. She would be calm. In control. He would never know.

Having made up her mind, she forced herself to go through the actions one by one. First slip out of the gold bikini. Second put on the dress. No time for a shower. Her skin was dry already. A spray of perfume. Then sandals. Where were the sandals?

She groped like an automaton in the bottom of the cupboard. Then the hair. Brush it. Leave it loose. No energy to tie it up. Make-up? She hovered near the mirror. She would show him. In control. A little lip-gloss. Liner. A touch of shadow. Now she was ready.

Like a sleep-walker she moved to the door, then with a quick gulping breath she made her way to the head of the staircase. Then she descended to the gathering below.

'Here she is!' It was Anna. There was an empty place halfway down the table. So many people, she thought, glancing at the familiar faces of the García Montada employees. So large an audience.

With a brilliant smile fixed to her face she swayed slowly across the terrace towards them all. There was a lull in the conversation as one by one the eyes followed the direction of Rodrigo's glance and swivelled to watch her.

She greeted first those nearest, then, as she moved along the rows to the top of the table where he sat with the dark woman on his right, she greeted others. Only when she drew level with Rodrigo himself did her smile falter.

Forcing herself not to cast even so much as the flicker of a glance towards the reproving presence of his fiancée, she said, 'Do forgive me, Rodrigo...' She paused. 'That is what you wanted, isn't it?' She paused again, eyes brilliant with repressed misery. 'I mean, forgive me for being so *late*.' She bestowed a smile on him, eyes dead beneath their superficial sheen, then, still the centre of attention, she moved calmly to the place reserved for her with the rest of the staff.

Little by little the conversation resumed. Anna, a slight smile of alarm on her face, tried unsuccessfully to catch her eye across the table. A waiter filled her glass. Chrissy kept the smile on her face. It was will-power pushed to its ultimate.

CHAPTER TEN

CHRISSY saw Rodrigo knock over a wine glass. The liquid flowed like blood over the white cloth. The fiancée gave a little cry. Her veil was back now revealing a plain, plump face, sharp brown eyes and scarlet lips. Gold hoops glinted in her ears and her glossy black hair was scraped back off her face and coiled in a tight bun at the nape of her neck. It looked so dark it was like black lacquer.

Chrissy tried not to hate her, even when she dabbed at a spot of wine on Rodrigo's sleeve with a lace-edged handkerchief and smiled possessively up at him. He took the handkerchief from her fingers and handed it to one of the maids. Another cloth was spread at their end of the table; things took up where they'd left off.

The man on her right was trying to engage her in conversation, struggling gallantly with her language when he realised she didn't speak his own. She forced herself to respond, tried to school herself not to let her glance stray continually to the far end where now there was a burst of merriment. Her glance was grasped by a sudden, piercing, ice-blue stare. At least *he* wasn't laughing. She averted her head, cutting off that fleeting contact.

When coffee was brought the guests scattered, some to the loungers, one or two, she was pleased to note, donning swimming gear, with plans to swim later on.

Chrissy wondered if Rodrigo was going to announce his betrothal. An old-fashioned word. Did it hint at a dynastic marriage after all? Was that supposed to make a difference to her feelings? She tried to imagine what

she would do if an announcement was made. Cause a
scene? Pretend it meant nothing? Offer her
congratulations?

Luckily she wasn't pushed to the test. Time went on.
No announcement was made. The afternoon turned to
evening. The fiancée smiled and smiled in a way that
didn't quite reach her eyes. Rodrigo wore the air of a
condemned man. Chrissy struggled among the ruins of
a shattered heart.

It was night now. The sun dropped like a red plum off
a tree. Little lights came on, covering the surface of the
water with wriggling snakes of gold. It was still hot.
Steamy. Fireflies danced. In the background was the
continual howl of night creatures. The swoop of bats.
Eyes that glinted and were gone. She imagined Rodrigo's
mother, for whom, like herself, the jungle was a threatening place, steeling herself not to be afraid. Their circle
of light and life and order seemed so small set against
that vast emptiness beyond the perimeter of the hacienda. Hadn't Miguel García understood this?

She drifted down to the paddock fence. Beneath the
soaring royal palms she felt something powerful take hold
of her. It was like a call, drawing her deeper into the
night. A wave of self-pity at the thought that he wouldn't
care a damn if she disappeared forever into that savage
maw brought a constriction to her throat. She turned,
blinded by it. He would not force her to do *that*. She
stumbled back towards the lights of the house.

They were walking towards her down the path. The
fiancée was fingering the gold brooch at her neck, hair
as sleek and black as ever. There was no way Chrissy
could turn back without being seen. She marched on,
spine straight, hoping that by the time they drew level

her face would be unmarked by that sudden access of grief that had overtaken her beneath the palms.

Now they had seen her. She saw Rod's lips tighten. Would they part and let her through, or would she be forced to step off the path so as not to hinder their progress? Her heart was bumping uncontrollably. Why are you doing this to me, García Montada? she cried inwardly.

They came to a halt a few paces in front of her as if waiting for her to go to them. Rod's face was still and stern, his eyes watching as if unsure what she was going to do. Maybe he thinks I'm going to fly at him with my nails and claw his face to ribbons? She took a deep breath and drew level.

'Chrissy.' He spoke first, his voice flat with pain. 'I didn't get chance to introduce you properly. Please——' there was a haunted look on his face '—Maria Carvela de Cana, Christine Baker.'

How drab her name sounded beside the exotic foreign one. The woman held out one hand, poker-straight.

'Maria speaks little English,' he said. Explaining away her silence, thought Chrissy, as they politely touched fingers.

'It's all right,' she replied, 'As you know, I don't speak much Portuguese.'

She turned to Rod. 'In the circumstances it's a good job she doesn't speak English. It means I can tell you what a louse you are.'

She gave him a brilliant smile and, still smiling, went on, 'In fact, it's very very lucky she doesn't understand, because in my opinion she's going to have to get very used to playing deaf and dumb with you around. No doubt you'll be running quite a household, Roddy darling. I hope you've warned her what a hot devil you are when it comes to trying to get other women into bed.

If you ask me she's got her time cut out with you on her hands, sweety. Rather her than me! She has my total sympathy. I only hope she's able to find solace elsewhere when the going gets really tough.'

Still smiling, she made to walk past him.

'Not so fast, honey,' he said, giving a bland smile that didn't reach his eyes but concealed the heavy-duty sarcasm he was indulging. 'You're not such a cold fish yourself, and if you will flaunt your beautiful, not to say delectable body at every turn, you shouldn't complain when you get a full-blooded response.'

'You snake!' she hissed.

'Listen to me,' he said more urgently. 'I've told you how I feel about you. I want you. I've wanted you since that first moment when I found you sleeping like a dryad in my forest. Nothing will change that. But I have to do this. It's the only way out. I've explained it to you. One of these days you'll understand.' He was speaking rapidly as if to get it all said, the sarcasm gone.

She felt her throat constrict. 'I'll never understand, Rod. You made it possible for me to stay, then you do this to me. I shall never forgive you.' Feeling her eyes beginning to glisten, she wished the couple would move apart and let her through.

Maria put a hand on Rod's arm *'Caro...?'* Her face was troubled.

'Si...' He put his hand over hers and stepped to one side. Chrissy barged through the gap and made her way blindly towards the house.

The dancing went on halfway through the night. She wondered if indeed the engagement had been announced and she had missed it for there was an air of celebration which only made her heartache worse. She sat up in her room, watching the inverted shadows of dancing couples on her ceiling. She had to get away, but how? She was trapped until Rod gave her the means to leave. No doubt after today he would be only too eager to send her home. He must have known she wouldn't stay when he was contemplating marriage to someone else.

'What do you want?' She turned her head. He had come inside without knocking and was closing the door behind him when she spoke.

'That's immaterial at this point,' he muttered hoarsely, coming across the room.

'Don't touch me!' She drew back against the balcony.

'I don't intend to.' He sat down in one of the chairs within. 'Come inside and sit down.'

'I'm happy out here.'

'Come inside, I said. I don't want all and sundry to know I'm in your room.'

'I bet you don't!'

'Would it be fair?'

'On whom?'

'Don't go round in circles. I've told you there is no choice. I'm not being unfair to you, if only you would try to see it!'

'Not unfair?' She lunged forward so she could see him. Her eyes were shining with unhappiness. 'You set up a peach of a contract for me then turn round and get yourself engaged to someone else. Is that fair?' There was no point now in pretending she didn't feel anything.

'It may not seem fair right now. But you are young. You think you're attracted to me—but it will soon fade. What is physical love after all?'

'How would I know?' she muttered, turning her head.

'No, that is another thing that makes it vital that we stop now before we get any deeper into this.'

She wondered how deep it was possible to get if this was only the shallows. 'All right for you to say—picking me up, putting me down. Why did you make me feel like this?'

'I can assure you, Chrissy, that was not my intention. If I had known you were going to feel as strongly as this I would have made jolly sure I kept my distance from the beginning.'

'You would? What wonderful self-control you have.'

'If it's any consolation it hasn't been easy. I should have been more determined.'

'Why weren't you?' she asked miserably, unable to keep the reproach out of her voice.

'You are right to blame me.' He paused. 'I am after all the one with the experience—I should have been more careful. But your feelings will pass, believe me. It is an infatuation, probably. Feelings of being in love are nothing.'

'How would *you* know? What gives *you* the right to tell me about my own feelings? How do you *know* how it feels to me?' She checked herself. She mustn't sound as if she was pleading. He was absolutely right. There was no future for them.

He was considering her words and now his voice deepened. 'I can assure you I do know. I know... But I did try to explain to you. You are from the same part of the world as my mother. You too would sicken here. Then you would want to leave. By then love would have deepened. You would strike at the very foundations of— of everything. It would be like trying to uproot one of the giant trees of the forest. It could be done, but the scar would remain forever——' He broke off impatiently. 'I can't do it! Be satisfied with that. This is how it must be!'

'Go to hell, then! Why come here at all? Get out of this room. Send me back to the city now! Tonight! Do you think I can bear to stay here with things like this between us?'

'You're being impractical. Even I can't summon a helicopter just like that.' He snapped his fingers.

'You mean the great Rodrigo García Montada can't do any single damn thing he chooses? My, you do surprise me!'

'The truth is I don't want to send you away yet. I had hoped...' He paused again. 'You know what I hoped. But I suppose that is all to ashes now?'

'You mean the contract?'

She saw him nod, his face a blur in the flickering light from the garden.

'Is it finished?' she asked. 'I don't see why that should come to ashes as well as—as well,' she corrected miserably. 'Gavin can take over. He doesn't want to but I'm sure he will. Or you can advertise for someone. There are plenty of people who'd leap at the chance.' Her lips twisted. 'You can even advertise for a female researcher, pretend you believe in equal opportunities, but don't forget to ask them to send a photo first. Then you can vet them properly!'

'This bitterness does not become you.'

'What the hell else do you expect me to feel? You led me to think there was the beginning of something real between us. I really started to believe in you—the least I believed was that you wanted me...that you felt something of some sort...' She didn't know how to go on because she couldn't see his expression. That was what made the whole thing worse. He was sitting very still. Watching her so coldly. As if in judgement. His face a blur. Eyes just two dark hollows.

Then he spoke and his voice was gruff and the words ran on swiftly as if in a hurry to get it over. He said, 'I *care*, God how I care—you *must* know that! But you will not, cannot settle for less than marriage. I understand that. I respect you for it. But you already know that is the one thing I cannot give you. Chrissy, Chrissy, can't you understand? I *cannot* marry you.'

'You're so good at the persuading game. I suppose that's what comes with experience.' She gave a cocky laugh. 'Of course you *respect* my reasons for saying no—but it doesn't stop you from making the attempt—I mean in trying to buy me!'

'*Buy* you?' He sounded incredulous.

'What else would you call it? However you dress it up it would come down to the same thing. Your job offer comes with a hefty grant. I'd be neatly tied by a contract. An apartment comes along with the appointment, so I gather from your outline. How long would it be before you managed to persuade me to m-make love with you?' Her voice was beginning to tremble under the strain of anger and betrayal. 'How could I fight with all that stacked against me? It would be so *easy* for you. The perfect plan! I would be set up in a little flat in a strange city, in a country I didn't know——'

'But the apartment is part and parcel of the job!'

'Naturally. And how long would it be before you were a frequent visitor? Whenever you got bored with your wife you'd just happen to come to town "on business" no doubt—very neat, very convenient.'

'And could you see yourself doing that for me?' He was white-lipped.

'*Degrading* myself? Parading around like a scarlet woman? Are you *mad*?' Her vehemence was all the stronger for a reason she knew very well—temptation had flaunted itself, and, though she had rejected it, a voice still insisted that she could have her heart's desire if only she would compromise.

She retreated to the balcony and turned her back but she could tell he had risen from his chair inside and followed her out. When she turned he was standing in the doorway.

'You have no opinion of me at all, do you?' His expression was strained. 'Maybe I'm a fool to expect you to know what is going on in my heart. I am trying to see it from your point of view. How it must look to you. But I cannot.'

'That's maybe the reason for the so-called curse on your family's marriages,' she said sharply.

He lifted his head.

'Think about it,' she advised with a bitter smile.

He was closer now, not touching, but near enough for her to feel the old chemistry at work. 'I'm not going to touch you,' he told her roughly, reading her mind. 'But you must tell me what you mean.'

'It's so obvious it doesn't need explanations,' she replied with a weary shake of her head.

'I am obviously very stupid. Go on. Explain.'

'You don't understand? Look——' She flung one arm out towards the jungle. 'How does it seem to you?'

He looked out into the night. 'It is rain forest,' he said at last. 'Income. Also very beautiful. Very mysterious. It has its secret life...'

'Go on. How would it seem to an English woman, alone in this country with your autocratic father as sole companion?'

'What?'

'Yes, I read your father's notes, the family book, it was there, in the library.'

'It is not secret, you had a right to read it. I asked you to, but what do you mean?'

'Imagine how she felt?'

'Autocratic, you said?'

'Wasn't he?'

There was a pause. Reluctantly Rodrigo admitted it was true. 'A bit of a tartar, yes,' he half smiled. 'A bear, would you say? But underneath a romantic, and madly in love with my mother.'

'But did she know that? She was very young when she married him. They lived alone here. Nothing happened from day to day. I've seen her diaries. "Again nothing. Miguel has his land. Days pass. I am buried alive. Has the whole world forgotten we exist?" That's a cry from the heart. So of course she sat at that window looking out at the road, desperate I should think to see another human being walking along it who wasn't an employee of her husband.'

Rodrigo's face was white as he considered what she was saying.

She went on. 'If some of the brides who married into the Montadas felt like that of course things turned to tragedy.'

'Surely that is what I am telling you? Here you would always hate it.'

'*Fear* it,' she said softly. 'Fear the rain forest. Its hidden dangers. Its secrets. Its boundlessness. Its massive loneliness...'

'So,' he replied after a short pause, 'hate, fear, it comes to the same thing. There would be no future for us.'

'I hadn't realised we were still discussing that topic,' she said icily, drawing back. 'I was simply trying to point out that if you want understanding you have to try to understand others too. If you want someone to be happy, you don't pretend their feelings don't exist, you *listen* to them, you *share* with them and you solve problems by sharing them. If only your father had listened to your mother, she would have stayed with him until the end. She loved him. It tore her heart out to leave him. She wanted to take you with her but knew that would destroy him more than her own leave-taking. She would have come back to him too. But he wouldn't hear of it. His pride was hurt. He refused to ask her to return. She died thinking he didn't want her back.'

'He was a proud man with an unforgiving streak.' His face was sombre.

Stubborn like you? she wanted to ask, but what was the point? It was over with them even before it had begun. He had made up his mind about that.

'Thank you, Chrissy. You've helped me see things in a different light. I must ensure that it doesn't happen——'

'Between you and your fiancée?' she cut in. 'Well, I'm sure she's quite a different person. I should think she might not even notice the enormous emptiness out there. I would imagine her interests are entirely domestic.'

'You are a bitch, aren't you?' His eyes kindled.

'No. I didn't mean it like that. She strikes me as someone who will be very content to run your household and bear your children and,' her voice thickened, 'and all that sort of thing,' she finished lamely.

'You are right, of course. That's why I chose her. She is excellent wife material.'

'I expect I missed the announcement,' she said dully.

'Not at all. Nothing has yet been announced. We are at the stage of discussion. But I felt I must tell you as soon as possible as I didn't want you to feel I was deceiving you. Maybe giving false hopes.' He shrugged. 'I knew too it was one way of severing this finally between us because, contrary to what you imagine, I knew you would never contemplate a relationship with me that would turn you into some sort of scarlet woman. And as that is also what I wanted to avoid, this seemed a way of extricating both of us.'

'A way of warning me off?' Her heart broke. 'How neat.'

'Quite so. It puts me out of bounds, does it not?'

'Maria would be very flattered to know all this,' she managed to get out.

'She has the story in its entirety,' came the surprising response. 'I have concealed nothing from her. Not even my—my desire for you. Although,' he gave a humourless laugh, 'it would have been impossible to conceal the effect you had on me this afternoon when you rose from the waters like a sea goddess—she would have had to be almost blind not to understand my reaction.'

'I thought you were angry with me——'

'My sweet...I *wanted* you...' A momentary gentleness came into his voice but he forced it away. 'If you must know I longed to be angry with you. As I do now,' he went on. 'Alas, it isn't possible. This would all be so much easier if we could part with rage in our hearts...'

He seemed to pull himself together with an effort and his voice levelled. 'Luckily Maria willingly accepted the fact that this will be a marriage—how do you say?—a dynastic marriage? She understands that. Welcomes it. She will become even more wealthy. It is quite usual for families like ours. She is also grateful for the opportunity it offers to return some fellow's ring which she has been wearing to little purpose for quite some time.'

He went on, 'A love-match, so I am to understand, at least on her side. Feeling she has waited long enough, she suggested this face-saving solution after I told her...' He paused then added irritably, 'It is not good to be a spinster at the age of twenty-eight, she feels. Her family will welcome our decision.'

'How cold you both are.'

'When passions are liable to consume those involved
it is wise to become like ice.' Despite his words his voice
shook, revealing how thin the ice was.

But Chrissy was too consumed with emotion to hear
it. 'You mean that underneath that calculating façade
of yours there's a heart pulsing with human blood? Ha!'
The strain of continuing was becoming too much. She
could feel her limbs trembling. She groped forward in
the darkness to find a chair. His hand came out, gripping
her by the arm.

'Chrissy...'

She could feel the blood throbbing through the tips
of his fingers, calling up a response in her that made her
gasp, and although he didn't say anything else that one
word uttered with such intensity seemed to express all
the violence of his desire.

'Don't, please don't——!' she cried against the side
of his head as their bodies searched for each other in
the darkness. It was like a home-coming to feel his arms
pull her into their warm circle at last.

She clung to him, touching his hair, his face, his lips.
'Oh, Rodrigo...' she moaned. Her mouth searched and
met his as he searched at the same instant for hers, then
they were spiralling down into the consuming depths
where desire was the only law, his mouth hotly plun-
dering, hers yielding without restraint.

He pulled her into the velvety darkness inside the
room, his mouth still burning in a fever against hers,
forcing her to respond to every quivering movement as
he coaxed her to yield him everything. But even when
his fingers sought the honeyed skin within the confines
of her dress he found no resistance, only yearning and
loving, as in an instant, shyly and helplessly, she surrendered at once her heart, her soul, every small response alive with love and trust.

With a stifled exclamation he stilled her beneath his more experienced touch, caressing her in a way that calmed and steadied her erupting wildness.

'No, we can't do this. Not like this. Don't, angel, be still.' He held her face steady between his palms. 'We mustn't. You would hate me. Nothing has changed... It cannot be. Stop now.'

Slowly calming her, his words penetrating the haze of desire that obscured her usual control, she was aware of his great strength supporting her, but, inexperienced as she was, she knew that a part of him was still resisting the need for control, every muscle throbbing with the desire to take her. Above it all his will of steel, tightening its hold, bringing him to a pulsing state of tension, a point of balance that still needed only one push to send it out of control.

Words rose to her lips, feverish words prompting her to plead with him, to demand his loving, to exact it when she knew it was almost hers, but she forced them back. 'I can't go on without you,' she told him instead. 'If you love me, say you love me. That will have to do. But if you don't then let me go.'

'I want to hold you and touch you——' he murmured hoarsely against her mouth.

'Say you love me if you do,' she pleaded. 'Tell me if it's true...'

She tried to trace the contours of his face in the darkness with her lips. If only she could see the expression in those sky-blue eyes, but they were like two pits as endless as night in the mask of his face, giving nothing away.

He didn't say the words she wanted to hear. They were the only words that would make the loving and the leaving bearable. Someone once said, better to have loved and lost than never to have loved at all. And she clung

to him, desperate to hear him tell her that one thing that
would make the sacrifice worthwhile, because she would
know that the anguish it left would be shared.

'I want to hold you all night,' he repeated instead in
that hoarse whisper. 'I want to love you till dawn. I want
to take you to heaven and back. But we know we cannot.
Don't fight it, angel. We cannot. Not here. Not like this.
Not in this house at this time. Tomorrow I would hate
myself. You would feel betrayed when it was time to part.
To make love would make it impossible ever to be together again——'

'How should we ever be together again?' she whispered hopelessly.

'When you take over at the lab——'

'You can't imagine I could become your employee
after this?' she breathed, scandalised, tearing her lips
from their melting contact with the smooth muscles of
his shoulder.

'Now yes, surely it *will* be possible?' he groaned. '*Now*.
If we do nothing to regret. But after knowing each other,
it would be impossible.'

'You believe that?'

'I know it would.'

'No, I mean, do you believe I could work for you...?'

'You *must*. I cannot let you go altogether! At least
we would have that——'

'What for? To carry the torment a stage further?' She
was trembling as she tore herself away from his embrace. 'How do you think I could live, knowing you
were loving someone else? Do you imagine I have such
control over my emotions?'

'You will forget this madness in time. We will feel differently. We will be calm. This craziness will be simply
a memory——'

'*Will* it? You mean, as it will be for *you* perhaps?'
She forced his hands away again, making herself do it
in order to gain some strength. 'So *that's* why you won't
say you love me? Because you know for you it's only
lust. It's an animal hunger that you'll satisfy some other
way until it fades.' Her fingers came to her mouth.
'You've always known what you felt for me would come
to nothing. I've been too blind to see it. I thought—oh,
how stupid I am. How naïve! It must make you smile
to discover how inexperienced I am—mistaking plain lust
for love!'

Unable to bear the knowledge that even now, magic
though his touch had been, powerful because of his un-
satisfied desire, it had been merely an animal reaction,
with nothing finer in it, she groped blindly for the door.

'I kept seeing clearly, over and over again, how you
just wanted me in order to add to your collection,' she
bit out, 'but I shut my eyes to the truth because—because of what I felt. I thought—I hoped you felt it too...'

The world was a nightmare with such traps in it. How
could the touch of one man spell heaven when all it came
down to was the hunger of one animal for another?

She ran out into the corridor, his shout ringing in her
ears. Blinded by despair, she blundered down the stairs,
scarcely caring whether she bumped into anyone on the
way, until, with a recklessness she had never felt before,
she went plunging off into the terraced gardens, running,
blindly running, until she felt the night close round her
and the hacienda with its painful memories recede.

Far enough away from the garden lights to go unob-
served, she slowed at last, wandering in blind torment
along the pathways threading the margin of the forest.
As the trees closed round it was strangely silent as if her
presence had made the wild creatures wary of betraying
themselves. It lulled her into a feeling of security. She

half imagined that by rejecting the human world the natural one welcomed her as an accomplice.

Without conscious aim she pushed her way deeper between the close-packed trees, creepers and liana twining round her wrists, brushing her face, swinging silently shut behind her. She was scarcely aware of what she was doing.

Then she realised she was lost. At first she didn't care. Nothing mattered now. Shut out of Rodrigo's life, she belonged nowhere. Dense vegetation blocked her at every turn. She had to force her way through the thick columns. Eyes glimmered out of the darkness following her steps. Little by little she heard the night sounds start up again—a whirr, a click, a sudden scream close by, then more distant cries, eerie, half human. The mating calls of countless insects gathered in violent chorus. Soon the noise rose on all sides, a cacophony to match the discord in her heart. It was as if the rain forest, satisfied she was one of them, was drawing her in to its endless, inhuman loneliness.

Pushing at a barrier of vegetation, she felt a sting on her shoulder. She turned with an exclamation. Then it was as if unseen fingers fastened round her throat. She stumbled, falling into deeper darkness. She was suffocating now in the damp, foetid atmosphere beneath the giant trees. Fear enveloped her, sending her scrambling back and forth in vain. There was no way out.

'Rodrigo!' she called, knowing he would never hear her.

Flesh crawled as something slithered over her foot. She failed to stifle a small shriek as the sound of some large unidentified creature crashed through the undergrowth towards her. It sent her running madly in the opposite direction. She tripped, falling full length. The thing was almost upon her. She could hear the harsh rasping of its breath. Horror sent her scrambling to her feet, running with the screams bottled inside until she hit another blind alley.

Then it was right behind her, its breath hot on her bare flesh.

'Chrissy! Stop!' Strong arms gathered her against a human form. The scent of vanilla enveloped her. The familiar, beloved voice was whispering over and over the words she had yearned to hear for so long. She knew she must be dreaming.

'Rodrigo!' she cried, pressing her face more desperately against the comforting bulk of his shoulder. She knew he would vanish in a moment, leaving her more alone than ever.

Then his lips inched over her skin. She heard the longed-for words again. 'I love you, Chrissy. I love you.' His lips pressed her temples, teaching her the shapes of the words he spoke, pressing their form against the pulse of her throat.

'I love you, Chrissy!' he repeated as if it was something he had newly discovered. 'Never, never, run from me again. Don't let me drive you away. Stay—stay where I can keep you safe forever.'

He held her protectively within the circle of his arms, lips pulsing feverishly over her face and as she heard the words she had despaired of hearing she felt the terrors of the night begin to fade.

His voice was hoarse when he started to piece the phrases together that told her what had been hidden in his heart. 'It was like death itself to see you run from me...' he whispered. 'The blackness without you! I never expected it to be like that. I refused to imagine life without you. I thought I could let you go. But I love you desperately...I always will. Never run away again, never, never. Now I've found you I won't lose you. I want to have you and hold you forever.'

The symphony of the rain forest was rising in full song on all sides as he added the sweet music of his love in words she had longed to hear. 'If the only way to keep you by my side is to make you my bride,' he told her, 'then that is how it must be... Say yes, my love. Say you'll stay forever.'

Unable to speak, she could only nod her assent. Her arms came up to lock themselves behind his neck. His lips were only inches from her own, rapidly confessing everything in his heart.

'I shall learn all the ways in heaven to make you happy living in the forest,' he vowed. 'It is as you say—we must try to understand each other. We will share all things. Our hopes, our joys, everything, and I shall keep all fear and sorrow at bay for you. I will make life a dream. We will have paradise here.'

Chrissy's heart began to sing. The fear that had sent her running towards the oblivion of the forest had been vanquished by the magic of his words. Instead of emptiness, she was surrounded by all the richness of being loved. He loved her. He said so. Paradise had already begun.

He made a solemn promise. 'I will give you everything I possess. My name, my heart, my love. You will be my bride.'

When they returned to the house, the guests were beginning to leave. They said goodbye to them, standing side by side on the steps. Chrissy's dress was a little stained, her hair in wild wood-nymph tendrils around her shoulders. Rodrigo had a lick of black hair hanging over his brow, making him look even more raffishly handsome than ever.

He stood with one arm round her shoulders, her hand resting in his—just as for three hundred years the García Montadas had posed on the same steps with the hands of their betrothed resting in theirs.

'To see you disappearing into the rain forest, being swallowed up by the darkness——' his voice sank to a hoarse whisper when they were at last alone '—it was a stark image of what the future would be like without you—the blackness, the emptiness... I saw myself living without you down all the dark years forever...'

She felt a shiver of fear run through her and forced herself to say the words that could bring the foundations of paradise to dust. 'But, Rodrigo, there is one thing...there is your promise to Maria.' She leaned against him as if it might be for the last time. When he had plucked her out of the nightmare forest she had forgotten everything but the healing balm of his kiss. She was shivering uncontrollably now.

He took her more firmly into his arms. 'Maria is no problem,' he began. 'She has been urging me to change my mind all day, ever since she saw my reaction as you emerged from the pool. She has been nagging me to put things right between us. It was I who insisted that what we had decided was right. If she could have spoken to you she would have explained how she felt. I spent most of the day trying to explain to her how strongly I felt that I would be wrong to persuade you to stay with me.'

He crumpled her hands between his own. 'But tell me, angel, tell me now, will you start to sicken for your own people? Will you sit in that little boudoir as my mother used to, longing to escape to the mists and cold of England?'

'Sometimes,' she smiled softly, 'and if it ever gets too much we'll both go back—together—and after a short measure of all that we'll come back home again—to our home in the forest.'

He kissed her, and she said, 'How could I want to leave my new-found land for good when everything I love is here?'

He turned her towards the house. 'Perhaps there are things about this almost engagement of mine with Maria that need explanation——' he began.

But at that moment they saw Maria herself crossing the hall, and when she saw them both she turned and hurried towards them. She was looking radiant. Gone was the worried expression she had worn earlier.

She moved swiftly, putting a hand on Rodrigo's sleeve. For one heart-stopping moment Chrissy thought that despite Rodrigo's reassurance she was coming to reclaim him. She imagined the whole nightmare starting up again, that his whispered vows in the forest had been her own desperate fantasy—but instead, Maria kissed him briefly on the cheek then stepped back with a beaming smile that took in at once their clasped hands.

'Caro.' She touched Chrissy lightly on the shoulder, then, her radiance unmistakable, she began to explain something rapidly to Rodrigo, shooting one or two shy glances in Chrissy's direction, and when she finished she gripped them both by the hands and to Chrissy said, 'It was all crazee—now is good, very good! Rodrigo tell you!' Then she turned and ran lightly up the stairs.

Rodrigo turned to her, 'The rumour of her marriage to me seems to have forced her errant fiancé to act. He rang here this evening demanding her immediate return to the city in order to fix a marriage date.' He laughed. 'I wanted to explain, she is an old family friend. We've known each other since the cradle. Her family hoped we would eventually marry, but neither of us took the idea seriously. When I told her I was being driven to madness by you and that it was impossible, she suggested marriage to solve both our problems. The reason she changed her mind about it was as I told you just now. She says she has never seen me in love before.'

His eyes deepened to cobalt. 'She was saying she didn't understand until she saw us together how much you mean to me.'

He lowered his lips. 'She said she's sorry if she made you sad.'

It took a moment or two for his words to sink in, then Chrissy threw her arms around his neck but her kiss was not for his cheek. Their lips met as he murmured, 'Stay with me, angel. Stay by my side forever.'

And when she lifted her lips, she replied, 'I will, my love. I will!'

**HARLEQUIN PROUDLY PRESENTS A
DAZZLING CONCEPT IN ROMANCE FICTION**

 One small town,
twelve terrific love stories

JOIN US FOR A YEAR IN THE FUTURE OF TYLER

Each book set in Tyler is a self-contained love story; together,
the twelve novels stitch the fabric of the community.

LOSE YOUR HEART TO TYLER!

Join us for the second TYLER book, BRIGHT HOPES, by
Pat Warren, available in April.

*Former Olympic track star Pam Casals arrives in Tyler to
coach the high school team. Phys ed instructor Patrick
Kelsey is first resentful, then delighted. And rumors fly about
the dead body discovered at the lodge.*

Janet Dailey®
Americana

Janet Dailey's perennially popular Americana series continues with more exciting states!

Don't miss this romantic tour of America through fifty favorite Harlequin Presents novels, each one set in a different state, and researched by Janet and her husband, Bill.

A journey of a lifetime in one cherished collection.

April titles   **#29 NEW HAMPSHIRE**
Heart of Stone

#30 NEW JERSEY
One of the Boys

Following the success of WITH THIS RING, Harlequin cordially invites you to enjoy the romance of the wedding season with

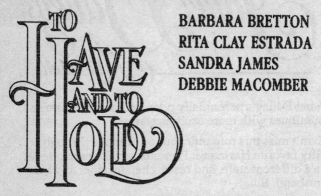

**BARBARA BRETTON
RITA CLAY ESTRADA
SANDRA JAMES
DEBBIE MACOMBER**

A collection of romantic stories that celebrate the joy, excitement, and mishaps of planning that special day by these four award-winning Harlequin authors.

Available in April at your favorite Harlequin retail outlets.

THTH

Harlequin Regency® *Romance*™

WHO SAYS ROMANCE IS A THING OF THE PAST?

We do! At Harlequin Regency Romance, we offer you romance the way it was always meant to be.

What could be more romantic than to follow the adventures of a duchess or duke through the glittering assembly rooms of Regency England? Or to eavesdrop on their witty conversations or romantic interludes? The music, the costumes, the ballrooms and the dance will sweep you away to a time when pleasure was a priority and privilege a prerequisite.

If you are longing for the good old days when falling in love still meant something very special, then come to Harlequin Regency Romance—romance with a touch of class.

RRG

Jackson: Honesty was his policy...
and the price he demanded of the woman
he loved.

THE LAST HONEST MAN
by Leandra Logan
Temptation #393, May 1992

All men are not created equal. Some are
rough around the edges. Tough-minded but
tenderhearted. Incredibly sexy. The tempting
fulfillment of every woman's fantasy.

When it's time to fight for what they believe in,
to win that special woman, our Rebels and Rogues
are heroes at heart. Twelve Rebels and Rogues,
one each month in 1992, only from
Harlequin Temptation!
